CONFRONTATION

"Just what are you trying to do, Lorie?" Leslie exploded, her whole face contorted with fury.

"Trying to do?" her sister repeated, her eyes widening in bewilderment.

"Don't play games with me, Lorie," Leslie snapped. "How'd you maneuver things so Brad would take you out to dinner tonight?"

"Oh, that," Lorie replied lightly. "Brad bet me a dinner I couldn't have my newspaper column ready by deadline. I won the bet."

Leslie felt silly and foolish. "I'm sorry, Lorie," she said quickly. "I should have known you wouldn't do anything to hurt me."

"I'd better get ready."

Leslie watched her sister run up the stairs. Then she eased herself into a chair in the steadily darkening living room and bit her thumb, hard, to keep from crying . . .

Bantam Books by Deborah Sherwood

THE YOUNG AND THE RESTLESS: THE STORY OF
    CHRIS AND SNAPPER
THE YOUNG AND THE RESTLESS: THE STORY OF
    BRAD AND LESLIE

THE YOUNG
AND
THE RESTLESS
THE STORY OF BRAD AND LESLIE

A novel by Deborah Sherwood
From the stories of William J. Bell

*Based on the Emmy Award-winning series
Created by William J. Bell and Lee Philip Bell*

THE YOUNG AND THE RESTLESS: THE STORY OF BRAD AND LESLIE
A Bantam Book | September 1976

ISBN 0-553-10115-3

Published simultaneously in the United States and Canada.

Bantam Books are published by Bantam Books, Inc. Its trade-
mark, consisting of the words "Bantam Books" and the por-
trayal of a bantam, is registered in the United States Patent
Office and in other countries. Marca Registrada. Bantam
Books, Inc., 666 Fifth Avenue, New York, New York 10019.

PRINTED IN THE UNITED STATES OF AMERICA

1

Had there ever been a more exciting time for the Brooks family? Leslie Brooks wondered as she sat alone at the kitchen table cracking walnuts for her special holiday cookies. She'd promised her youngest sister, Peg, she'd make them for the twelfth night party at the church and now, to her dismay, the twelfth night of Christmas was practically upon them and she'd only just remembered.

Christmas. She sat back in her chair and heaved a long satisfied sigh. Christmas was her favorite time of year. Since she'd been a little girl, she'd eagerly looked forward to the holiday season—all the bustle and the present-buying and the tree-trimming and the baking. All the caroling and the snow that crunched under your feet and the twinkly lights that transformed plain, ordinary Genoa City into a fairyland for a few enchanted weeks.

And this year, she mused pleasantly, the bustling and festive spirit in the Brooks home hadn't ended with the advent of the new year. Because on January 11, Les' second youngest sister, Chris, was getting married and there was a glorious wedding to prepare for. Although Chris was only nineteen years old, Les wasn't at all surprised that the pretty, down-to-earth girl who had never wanted to be anything but a homemaker was going to become the first of the four Brooks girls to be a bride. Peg, just turned seventeen, was too young even to be considered, and twenty-two-year-old Lorie, who'd

1

only just returned from four years of study at the American University in Paris, was far too much of a free spirit to settle down anytime soon. Beautiful, sophisticated, and extremely headstrong, Lauralee Brooks had come home insisting she was going to live life to the fullest before she tied herself down to a lot of housework and children running underfoot. And she'd spent most of last week talking about how foolish Chris was not only to allow herself to be tied down, but also to marry a struggling medical student who wouldn't be able to give her anything but poverty and deprivation for a long, long time. (Chris, to Les' delight, had merely smiled serenely and gone on making her wedding plans.)

As for Leslie herself, it had always been taken for granted by everyone that she wouldn't marry until much, much later because her whole life had been dedicated to a concert career since she'd first climbed upon a piano bench at the age of six and a half. Years of study—first here in Genoa City and then in New York at the Juilliard School of Music—and hours upon hours of practicing had left little time for partying and dating, not to mention falling in love.

"Don't worry, Les, darling," her father used to tell her encouragingly as she'd watch Lorie and Chris getting ready for an evening out on the town while she faced a night of Beethoven in an empty living room "the time will come when *they'll* be envious of *you*. When you become a famous pianist, the invitations will flow like champagne and the young men will flock around you so eagerly you'll have to beat them off with a stick."

What Stuart Brooks didn't know then was that Leslie hadn't actually minded not being able to join her sisters in the teenage social whirl. Shy, introverted, and by her own appraisal just plain dull, she'd always hated parties, and she was scared to death of boys. Boys had to be flirted with and toyed with and manipulated and managed, and how a girl did those things had remained one of the great mysteries of her young life. Not for one minute would she consider competing in the dating game with the smooth, pretty girls who knew all the little female wiles and tricks and used them with such bold assurance. She, thank you, would settle for what was to her mind the far-less-complicated role of musician.

Of course she was not unaware of the fact that, in spending all those hours at the piano, she was actually allowing herself to escape from a world she found frightening and overwhelming. But now, she reminded herself, her eyes growing soft and a happy glow creeping into her face, all the study and practice and dedication —for whatever reasons they had taken place—were about to pay off. In February—less than two months away—she, Leslie Brooks, was going to embark on a concert tour as soloist with the prestigious Mid-America Symphony Orchestra. And perhaps, she speculated as she indulged in thoughts about her new and thrilling life, her father's prediction of long ago would even come true. Perhaps if she became successful enough, men *would* begin to seek her favor.

The thought caused her mouth to twist into a wry smile. Because, incredibly, it was too late for that now! All the exciting young men from New York to San Francisco could fall at her feet and she wouldn't so much as glance at any of them. The family didn't know it, but Leslie had already met the only man in the world for her: a warm, wonderful, devastatingly handsome man named Brad Eliot who worked at the *Chronicle,* the popular and highly respected newspaper Stuart Brooks edited and published. Les had been seeing Brad quietly since last spring, when they'd started going for walks together and occasionally having dinner at Pierre's. (The fact that Brad lived in a tiny, dreary room above the restaurant had nothing to do with the seemingly furtive nature of their meetings. They weren't keeping their relationship quiet because there was anything *wrong* in it; on the contrary, Brad had yet to kiss Leslie in any but a brotherly way.) Those meetings, when they'd sit side by side on a park bench, not even touching, or when, after the dinner crowd had left

Pierre's, they'd sip wine together and talk about music and feelings and life, were so precious to her that she wanted them to remain just hers and Brad's for as long as it was at all possible.

Anyway, she reflected as she put down the nut-cracker and began to pick the nutmeats out of their shells, telling her parents about Brad would only cause concern. Although Stuart had employed Brad at the paper and had nothing but admiration for his work, Brad Eliot on a personal level was strictly taboo. Because the man who had arrived in Genoa City virtually penniless and sporting a deep, ugly scalp wound above his left ear last spring was a man with a highly suspicious past.

Stuart had first met him at Pierre's during the lunch hour, when Brad had, upon finishing a hearty repast, confessed to Pierre, the usually bouncy Frenchman who owned the place, that he had no money; none whatso-ever. Stuart, overhearing and filled with a newspaper-man's natural curiosity, had entered the ensuing fray and had paid his check. And, of course, a conversation of sorts had followed. Stuart, without much difficulty, had learned that the man was from somewhere out of town and had been mugged on his way to Genoa City. But, oddly enough, that was all. To this day, almost nine months later, Brad had refused to open up to any-one—Leslie included—about who he actually was or where he'd come from or what business he had been in before meeting Stuart so precipitously and joining the *Chronicle* staff. He had assured Stuart that he wasn't wanted by the police or involved in any trouble, and Stuart, seeing something of merit in him despite all odds, had taken him at his word and promised to ask no further questions.

Her father, Leslie felt certain, had enough faith in his discovery to accept at least a casual relationship be-tween Brad and one of his daughters. But her mother, Jennifer, was still convinced the man's past contained something sordid and quite horrible, and it was all she could do to force herself to be polite to him when she

ran into him at the newspaper office or when he came
to the house to see Stuart on business.

Oh, Mother, Leslie thought with a wistful smile, if
you only knew how much Brad Eliot has done for your
awkward, insecure eldest child. If you only knew how
much his interest in me has drawn me out of my shell
and given me confidence and made me want to be
a complete woman and not merely an artist who happens to be female.

She laughed quietly to herself as she remembered
the means by which he had accomplished those things:
the terrible moments in which he had accused her of
being afraid of life and of having forgotten she was a
woman. He insisted she made herself look as unattractive as possible, always wearing her long light-brown
hair pulled severely back from her face and twisted into
an untidy bun at the nape of her neck, going without
makeup, and always wearing jeans and an old shirt
instead of putting on something more feminine once in
a while. How, she recalled with amusement, she had
hated him at those times! How she had wanted to
scream at him and run away from him and be finished
with him forever! But, somehow, she had never done
any of those things. She had endured all his cruelties
stolidly, and eventually she had had the sublime joy of
seeing him eat some of his own sour words.

It had happened one day last summer, when he'd
taken her out to Lake Genoa and dared her to put on a
bikini he'd (rather brazenly, she'd thought) bought for
her. He'd long been insisting she was ten pounds overweight and buying her the bikini was, by his own subsequent admission, meant to shock her into realizing it
for herself and doing something about it.

"Wow! Was I ever wrong!" he'd gasped when she'd
uncharacteristically accepted the challenge and thrown
off her beach robe to stand before him, blushing, but
proud of her firm, ultrafeminine body. At that moment
Lesle had experienced a triumph far greater than any
she had ever known at the piano: the triumph of woman winning over man. And after that, his criticisms had

been tempered with a good deal more respect, and Les began to find she didn't mind them nearly so much. In fact, she began to listen to this incredible man more carefully, realizing for the first time that he was right about so many things and that he criticized not to hurt, but to help her.

Slowly, almost imperceptibly, she had begun to change. Her long, naturally wavy hair was loosened from its bun and allowed to flow luxuriously around her shoulders. The ugly, old-fashioned glasses she'd worn had been replaced, thanks to her father's generosity, by contact lenses. Her face, which she'd always considered plain, bore just enough carefully applied makeup to bring out her best features and gave her a healthy look that gave the lie to the fact that she spent most of her life indoors. And, although she still wore her old jeans for practicing, her closet now sported several flattering sports outfits and two or three softly clinging dresses.

Funny, she thought, not knowing whether she ought to be pleased or insulted, that although her family had noticed the change, they hadn't even imagined it could have been brought about as a result of a man's influence. They'd just assumed, in their simple, loving way, that the excitement and prestige of the coming concert tour had made Les want to spruce up a bit, and they were proud of her for wanting to look as well as she played when she stepped out onto that first stage in February.

"Hey, is this a private party or can anybody join?"

Les looked up to see her sister Lorie, looking fantastic in a skintight black jumpsuit, her glorious mane of chestnut hair cascading to her shoulders, standing in the kitchen doorway.

"Come on in," Les invited, thinking to herself how strange it was to have this gorgeous, vibrant creature back home after all this time. "I'm just getting ready to start the twelfth-night cookies."

Lorie went to the stove and gingerly touched the coffeepot. Finding it cold, she turned a low flame on under it. "Dad told me the orchestra's setting up rehearsal dates for you," she said conversationally as she searched the refrigerator for something to eat.

Les nodded. "Maestro Fautsch wants me in Chicago the week after the wedding to rehearse with the full orchestra."

"Sounds very exciting." Lorie flopped in a chair next to her and nibbled daintily on a piece of leftover fruitcake.

"It's a little different from all those afterdinner family concerts when we were kids," Les said with a wry smile. "Thinking back, it must have driven you up the wall, having to sit there night after night, listening to me play."

"Why do you say that?" Lorie put down the fruitcake and fixed her wide green eyes curiously on her sister.

"You had better things to do," Leslie answered without bitterness. "All your friends wanting you to go out." She sighed, and her voice held more pride than envy. "My sister—the most popular girl in school."

Lorie shrugged prettily. "Dad thought it was important for you to have an audience. And, obviously, he was right. Look what you've done with yourself!" She shook her head, as if the change in her sister were something bordering on the miraculous. "Whoever would've thought that scared, introverted little girl with the braces and horn-rimmed glasses would grow up to be a concert soloist with a symphony orchestra?"

Although the words were flattering, Leslie sensed something more behind them. "Lorie," she said, looking at her sister earnestly, "you *are* happy for me?"

A flicker of annoyance crept across Lorie's face. "Why wouldn't I be?" she asked defensively.

"It's just that you hadn't even mentioned my music and the concert tour until now."

The younger girl held up her hands in the charming gesture of helplessness she invariably used to get herself out of uncomfortable situations. "There's been so much going on since I came home," she said, sounding exactly like a little girl who'd been scolded for being late to dinner. "The holidays, the wedding—I guess I didn't get around to your music." She stopped and her face worked itself into a contrite pout. "Sorry about that, big sister."

Leslie nodded, appeased. "It was silly of me to wonder."

"Don't tell me you still need all that family reassurance?" Lorie stared at her, dumbfounded.

"I still have some of my old hang-ups," Leslie admitted. "But," she added, refusing to let her sister make her feel guilty about them, "I know I'm a lot better now."

The coffee began to boil and Lorie jumped up to pour it, but she deftly managed to keep the conversation going, turning her head several times in the direction of this sister of hers who had turned out to be such a surprise. "How did that happen?" she asked, seemingly genuinely interested. "You get professional help?"

"No," Les replied. And then she went on a little shyly, "But there is someone who did as much for me as any professional could have."

Lorie studied her from across the room. "You were lucky."

"I think so." Leslie met her eyes and smiled.

"Imagine," Lorie said with envy she could not hide, "being stuck here in Genoa City and still having all this happen to you."

Les laughed. "You make Genoa City sound so dull."

"Isn't it?" It was more of a challenge than a question.

"It wouldn't be for you if you'd just let people know you're home. The telephone would be ringing off the hook, just like it did in the old days."

Lorie put her cup on the table and slipped back into her chair, curling her long legs and bare feet under her. She leaned toward her sister. "Did that bother you in those days, Les?" she asked, frowning.

"That you were popular and I wasn't?" Les shook her head. "I couldn't have handled it. I was too shy."

There was a long moment of silence as Lorie stared at her, her catlike eyes taking in the hairdo, the makeup, the poise, the incredible self-assurance. "I have a feeling," she said slowly, her pink tongue flicking her lips as it always did when she was trying to figure something out. "It's not anything anyone's said. . . . Call it female intuition if you like. But . . . I think you have a man in your life."

Leslie, startled, didn't know how to reply. For months she'd wondered why no one had guessed the truth. And now Lorie, who had only just returned after four years of being away, had taken one long look at her and seen it written in her face.

"The family doesn't know," she told her after a moment's deliberation, suddenly feeling a compelling urge to confide in this glorious creature who knew so much more about life and love than she would probably ever know. "And for reasons of my own, I don't want them to."

"But I'm right?" Lorie probed, her eyes gleaming with interest.

Leslie looked down at the table and mumbled an embarrassed confession. "I'm . . . in love with him."

"Love?" her sister asked curiously. "Or one of those fun-and-games things?"

Leslie's head shot up and her discomfort vanished in a fervent desire to make her sister understand. "It's love," she assured her earnestly. "Very deep. Very real."

She didn't add that—so far, at least—all that deep, real love was strictly on *her* side. Brad Eliot had drawn her out, encouraged her, literally transformed her, but he had never once given her any reason to believe it meant anything except that he was genuinely interested in her as a friend. Whether it would ever be anything more, Leslie couldn't perceive. But admitting she was in love, actually saying the words out loud, filled her with sudden, unexpected determination.

Why should she merely sit back and *dream* of the man and confide her longings, schoolgirllike, to her sister? She was a grown woman now, and if she wasn't a raving beauty, she at least had enough femininity to put up a fight. Somehow, she must try and find a way to make Brad see her as more than just a friend, a way to make his eyes light up the way they had when he had looked at her that day at the beach.

She rose from the table and gathered the cooking utensils from their respective cupboards and drawers. I've been a shrinking violet long enough, she admonished herself as she dumped the flour into a mixing bowl. I may not be able to win Brad Eliot—but if I don't try, I'll hate myself as long as I live.

So absorbed was she in these determined thoughts, she didn't even notice when, smiling enigmatically, Lorie drained the last of her coffee and quietly crept out of the kitchen.

2

Brad Eliot sat in the old, worn easy chair in his little room above Pierre's and studied the exquisitely engraved invitation that had been lying on top of his chest of drawers for the past two weeks.

MRS. ELIZABETH FOSTER AND MR. AND MRS. STUART R. BROOKS INVITE YOU TO SHARE IN THE HAPPINESS OF THEIR CHILDREN, CHRISTEN LEIGH AND WILLIAM JOSEPH, AS THEIR LIVES ARE JOINED IN MARRIAGE. FRIDAY, JANUARY 11, AT FOUR O'CLOCK IN THE AFTERNOON. CHURCH OF OUR SAVIOR, GENOA CITY.

Brad smiled as he read the words for what was perhaps the third or fourth time. "Mrs. Elizabeth Foster and Mr. and Mrs. Stuart R. Brooks invite you . . ." It was the first formal invitation he'd received since he'd arrived in Genoa City last April, and, somehow, it pleased him more than he'd thought possible. For the first time in longer than he cared to remember he felt as if he belonged, as if he were an entity and not the mysterious man with the murky background who had been thrust upon the Genoa City citizens without warning, and with nothing to recommend him but an honest face and a pleasing personality that seemed to inspire faith despite his refusal to reveal anything about himself other than his name and the fact that he was not a criminal.

Although he'd established himself as a person of

rather extraordinary natural talent at the *Chronicle* and was generally looked up to by other members of the staff, he'd made few real friends in these past months. There was Pierre, of course, his landlord and the owner of the restaurant downstairs, with whom he spent many a companionable night after closing hours having a drink and talking. Pierre, like Brad, was a private man, and although the Frenchman's past was not the secret Brad's was, the two men found a sense of oneness in each other and had formed a friendship that was solid without encroaching upon the other's wish for privacy.

Brad was also a good friend and confidant of Pierre's pretty, new wife, Sally. Before her marriage Sally, poor, uneducated, wanting so desperately to better herself and raise her status in life, had been known to take impulsive action she later came to regret, and she was misunderstood and even heartily disliked by those who hadn't taken the trouble to learn that she was misguided rather than a bad person. But Brad had a genuine liking for her, and he had become almost like a brother to her, listening to her and encouraging her when she seemed filled with despair and frustration, offering a strong shoulder for her to cry on when she couldn't hold back the tears, giving carefully weighed advice whenever it was wanted or needed. And lately, he was happy to say, the girl seemed to have pulled herself together and come to terms with the life she had fought with such agonizing results for so long.

Finally, of course, there was Stuart Brooks, Brad's boss at the paper and—he acknowledged it readily—his Genoa City mentor. Brad had developed a deep liking and respect for the *Chronicle*'s editor and publisher, not only because Stuart had been willing to take a chance on him but because he had always found him a fair and honest man who had kept his promise not to ask Brad any further questions about his former life.

Unfortunately, Brad reflected as he put the invitation back atop his chest of drawers, the same could not be said for Stuart's wife. Jennifer Brooks, though never overtly impolite, was distant and unmistakably cool whenever she happened to encounter Brad at the *Chronicle* office. He supposed he couldn't blame her for mistrusting him, especially since she was the mother of four attractive daughters, but he couldn't help wishing she'd at least keep an open mind about him.

What would she think, Brad wondered ponderously, if she knew how often I see her oldest daughter? Brad had first met Leslie when he'd gone to the Brooks home to see Stuart on business and had inadvertently wandered into the living room, where he'd found her practicing the piano. She had looked abominable that day, with her old-maidish hairdo, her outdated glasses, and those old jeans and sloppy shirt that totally disguised what he'd later learned was a beautiful figure. But something about her, something about the shy, uncertain way in which she spoke when she discovered he was in the room, appealed to the humanitarian in him. Though her musical talent was obvious even to him, her quiet, ingenuous manner seemed to imply that she was unsure, if not completely unaware of it. He'd spoken only a few words to her that day, but from time to time after that she would stop in at the newspaper office, and slowly a unique friendship had begun to develop.

There were no dates, really. Just long walks in the park, during which Brad tried hard to draw her out and make her aware of herself both as a person and as an artist, and an occasional dinner at Pierre's. And then, Brad remembered with an appreciative smile, there had been that day at the lake, when Les had made the first step in coming out of her shell, standing before him laughing, wearing that bikini that showed off the most dazzling figure he'd ever seen in his life and mocking him for daring to say she was ten pounds overweight. It had been then, he guessed, that he realized he enjoyed Leslie as a woman as well as someone he wanted to help.

Still, there was no romance between them, any more than there had been between him and Sally Rolland. Leslie was all wrapped up in her music. Although he knew she enjoyed the time they spent together, there

could be no doubt that a brilliant concert career was
what Leslie Brooks wanted out of life. And Brad . . .
well, Brad didn't know *what* he wanted.

He looked at his watch. Eleven o'clock. The
whole day stretched ahead of him. Sometimes he wished
he were required to work on Saturdays like some of the
other guys down at the paper. Because, despite the
way he'd settled into this new life of his, he still had
little to do to fill his leisure time. In fact, those casual
dinners and walks with Les were about the *only* things
that filled it. He ran a hand through his thick, dark hair.
Maybe he should call her now. They could spend the
day together, perhaps have lunch and do a little shopping. Yes, he decided, congratulating himself for having thought of it, a day with Les would be very pleasant.

She answered the phone in the Brooks home herself, and her eager young voice filled him with warmth
and made him glad he'd called.

"I have a request," he told her a little apologetically,
realizing it was the first time he'd ever asked her help
in anything.

"Oh?" Les sounded surprised.

"Can you help me find a wedding present?"

The voice on the other end was pleased. She was
very close to Chris and he knew shopping for her
would be more of a joy than a chore. "Of course," she
agreed brightly.

"I'll pick you up." When only awkward silence
greeted this statement, Brad remembered with cha-
grin that she never liked him to call for her. "You'd
rather meet me," he amended, resigned but disappointed.

Leslie seemed relieved. "Yes."

They agreed to meet at Pierre's in half an hour,
and she arrived on time, looking happy and pretty, her
face ruddy from the January air, her eyes sparkling
like lights on a Christmas tree.

"Why wouldn't you let me pick you up?" Brad

asked, realizing she'd had to stand in the cold and wait for a bus.

"I thought it would be easier for you if I met you." She rubbed her hands and stamped her feet to shake the snow off her boots.

"Is that the only reason?" He looked at her, hard.

"Why else?" Her voice was casual and she busied herself with removing her coat and muffler.

"Because," Brad replied, his dark eyes searching her face for the answer he knew was there, "you don't want your family to know we see each other like this."

Leslie shrugged. "It's our business, isn't it?"

"True," Brad was forced to admit.

"Then why not keep it to ourselves?" She had seated herself at the table now and was studying the menu with exaggerated intensity. "I think . . ." she mused thoughtfully, "I'd like an omelet." She looked up at him and smiled disarmingly. "With mushrooms."

Remembering the time, not so very long ago, when she'd become embarrassed and tongue-tied whenever he'd tried to probe into her head, he had to applaud her newfound self-assurance—however infuriating it might be at the moment—and her easy way of changing a subject she didn't care for to one of her own choosing. "You've come a long way in the last few months, Leslie," he told her admiringly, pulling his chair up and leaning toward her across the red-and-white-checked tablecloth. "You're ready for the great new year that's just started."

Leslie leaned back in her seat and released a long, wistful sigh. "I hope you're right," she answered softly.

"I know I'm right. A concert career won't be just a dream anymore. It will be a reality. The music world will accept you as the accomplished artist you are."

She leaned toward him then, her eyes glowing. "You make it sound so wonderful."

"It *will* be wonderful. Because you'll have made it come true on your own. I'm very proud of you, my friend."

"Thank you, Brad." Les' whole face reflected the pleasure she felt in his words. She would never be one to shrug off compliments lightly, no matter how famous she became.

"Let's drink a toast," he suggested impulsively when Pierre had brought them some steaming hot cider in brass mugs. "To you and to what's in store for you." He lifted his mug. "Fame. A whole world to explore and to win. Confidence in yourself. Pleasure in your accomplishments!"

As they drank, their eyes held. Anyone watching them from across the room would have been sure that these two young people who generated such warmth and intensity of feeling were drinking, not to a career, but to a beautiful love affair.

While her sister was out shopping, Lorie Brooks was curled up on the sofa in the living room, idly leafing through a fashion magazine. But, although the holiday fashions were interesting, she couldn't keep her attention from wandering with every turn of the page. She'd been back from Paris for almost a month now, and she still couldn't get over all that had happened in her absence.

Her younger sister Chris was getting married. Lorie didn't know why that should surprise her—old-fashioned Chris had always maintained that the only thing she wanted in life was a husband and family. But little Chris, a *wife!* It just didn't seem possible. She was getting a groovy guy, though, Lorie had to admit with an appreciative smile. Snapper Foster might be poor and have a lot of years of struggle ahead before he could give much to Chris in the way of luxuries, but he sure was mighty attractive! Lorie could almost understand her sister's action. A good-looking, undeniably masculine guy like Snapper just might be worth starving with.

And Les! The change Lorie had found in her older sister was more surprising than the wedding news. It wasn't only that Leslie had been chosen as soloist with the Mid-America Symphony that knocked Lorie for a loop. It was the way she had blossomed from a drab old maid to a confident, pretty, ebullient young woman. Although Les had been surprised when Lorie had suggested a man was responsible for the change, Lorie knew perhaps better than anyone that there was only one thing that could bring a girl out of herself like that. And the man who was responsible for bringing out a drudge like Leslie must be one hell of a special guy.

When Leslie had first admitted there *was* someone, Lorie had been dying of curiosity about him. But Les had refused to say anything about him, not even his name, and she'd had her antennae out ever since, hoping to pick up some sort of clue as to his identity.

She suspected she might have latched on to something earlier this afternoon when, while helping her mom and Peg sort out the wedding presents, Peg had suddenly mentioned something about hoping "that groovy mystery man, Brad Eliot" would show up at the church.

"Peg," Lorie had asked her, intrigued, "why do you call this Mr. Eliot the 'mystery man?'" She'd heard Dad had a new man by that name working for him at the paper, but she'd never relized there was anything mysterious about him.

"What else would you call him?" Peg had replied matter-of-factly. "No one knows anything about him."

Lorie had frowned. "How can that be?" she'd asked, puzzled. "He works for Dad."

"Yeah, but Dad doesn't know anything about him either." Peg turned away to pull a big silver serving dish out of its box. "On his way to Genoa City, he got mugged," she added, as if that were a natural explanation.

"Mugged?" Lorie had been stunned. She'd never known anyone who'd been mugged.

"Yeah. They stole his car . . . his money . . . all his valuables."

"Your father met Mr. Eliot at Pierre's, when he didn't have money to pay for his meal," Jennifer had put in, seeing Lorie's deepening interest. "He gave him a job on the paper, and now he's Stuart's right-hand man."

"Do I detect a little disapproval in your tone, Mom?" Lorie had asked. Her mother wasn't usually this cool and terse when describing people.

Jennifer had smiled guiltily and heaved a disturbed sigh. "Your father says he's brilliant in his work," she replied slowly. "And I've read enough of it to know he is. But he's always refused to say a word about his background. We don't even know where he's from."

Lorie had pursed her lips and her brow wrinkled slightly. "Doesn't sound like Dad—taking a chance on a man he knows nothing about."

"Wait till you meet him!" Peg told her enthusiastically. "Anybody would take a chance on Brad."

Jennifer had patted her youngest daughter's shoulder and shaken her head doubtfully. "I invited him to the wedding because Stuart and Chris both wanted him. But I still have reservations."

"Well!" Lorie had declared, her eyebrows lifting and her eyes glittering with interest. "It all sounds very intriguing."

Since then, she'd been thinking about that conversation and the one she'd had with Leslie that night in the kitchen. A mysterious man in Leslie's life, one whose name she refused to reveal, a man she didn't even want her parents to know about. A mystery man who worked at Dad's paper, a man with no known background whom her mother distrusted and even disliked. Could there be a connection?

The sound of a car pulling up outside jolted her thoughts. It couldn't be her parents and Peg coming back; they'd left only an hour or so ago. And Chris would be out with Snapper till who knew what time. Lithe as a cat, she sprang from the sofa and hurried to the front window. Standing pressed against the wall, her head turned sideways, she could see out of the side of the drapery without having to pull it back and call attention to herself.

A man—tall, well-built, very good-looking—was helping Leslie out of a car. Together, they walked up the sidewalk, Les, to Lorie's continuing amazement, laughing and talking animatedly. When they reached the porch, Lorie dashed back to the sofa and picked up a magazine, pretending to be absorbed in every word. She heard the front door open and Leslie's voice, alive, vibrant, ringing through the hallway.

"Hey, this was fun!" She gave a joyous little laugh.

The man's voice was deep and warm. "I enjoyed it, too. See you soon?"

"At the wedding."

"Yes." The man's voice became lower. "Good night, Leslie."

" 'Night, Brad."

Lorie's mouth curved into a small, satisfied smile as she heard the door close. So! The pieces *did* fit! Brad Eliot was the mystery man in Les' life. Not hearing Leslie's footsteps either coming into the living room or going upstairs, she quietly rose and wandered out to the entranceway. There she saw her sister standing before the hall mirror, studying her reflection wonderingly, as if unable to believe that this glowing, highly attractive young woman was really Leslie Brooks.

"Les?" Lorie's voice was soft, but Leslie started at the sound of it.

"Lorie! I thought everyone was at the twelfth-night party at the church."

Lorie gave a sardonic grin. "Now really, big sister, can you just see *me* at a church party?"

"Oh," Leslie chided lightly, "I don't think you're as bad as you pretend to be." She began to pull at her muffler and remove her coat.

"The man you're in love with, Les . . ." Lorie began tentatively.

"Yes?" Leslie whirled around and looked at her

with frightened eyes, like a deer that's been stalked by a hunter and knows it's been found.

"It's . . ." Lorie bit her lip as if afraid to go on. "It's Brad Eliot, isn't it?"

There was a moment's silence as their eyes met, Lorie's questioning and intent, Leslie's doubtful and uncertain. Then Les nodded, and a tiny smile played across her lips. "Please, Lorie, don't say anything about it to anyone. Because Brad doesn't have the slightest idea."

Lorie's face was expressionless as she studied her sister. "Don't worry about it, Les," she promised earnestly. "It'll be our secret."

Les reached out an arm and pulled her to her in a grateful hug. "I won't," she declared firmly. "I know I can trust you."

Lorie returned the hug and smiled. "You can," she assured her.

But the smile turned to a thoughtful frown as Leslie hung her coat in the closet and sailed blissfully up the stairs.

3

On January 11, Chris Brooks was married to William "Snapper" Foster in one of the most beautiful and touching ceremonies Genoa City had seen in a long time. First, spectators seated in the pews of the charming little church of Our Savior were treated to the sight of the bride's sisters. Leslie, Lauralee, and Peggy Brooks, looking pretty as three pictures in their graceful long gowns of pale blue as they made their way down the flower-banked aisle. Then Jill Foster, Snapper's younger sister and Chris' maid of honor, began the slow, majestic walk, and many a comment was made about what a lovely addition she was to the already blooming Brooks family.

And then came the most impressive moment of all—the emergence of Chris herself from the vestibule at the back of the church, radiant in her white gown of tulle and lace, affectionately clutching the arm of her proud, loving father. But, although all eyes were on her, it was plain that Chris had eyes for only one—the darkly handsome young man who stood so eagerly at the altar, next to his brother and best man, Greg Foster.

Reverend Martin, who had known the bride since she was a baby, performed the ceremony with dignity and warmth, reading a touchingly appropriate scripture from First Corinthians and then offering the wedding vows in a deep, resonant voice. And after that, tradition gave way to Chris and Snapper's own originality, and their friends and relatives smiled their approval as the young couple simultaneously lighted a tall candle wreathed in pine and holly as a symbol of their new oneness and Reverend Martin explained that the gesture would be repeated on each anniversary as a reminder of the vow they made this day. Then, as the candle flickered and danced, they removed two longstemmed red roses from a nearby vase and offered them to their parents as a symbol of their love and gratitude.

And when they left the church as man and wife—Chris glowing with happiness, Snapper proud and protective—everyone agreed they were almost like a couple in a storybook.

Wonders will never cease, Stuart Brooks told himself the following Monday as he dabbed the shaving cream off his chin and splashed after-shave on his face and neck. The year that had just come to an end had been a year of surprises, what with Chris deciding to marry so young—and, he reflected with a sigh, against his wishes—and Leslie's being chosen soloist with the Mid-America Symphony. But at the moment he had to admit that nothing had surprised him so much as the behavior of his second daughter, Lorie, since she had returned from Europe.

She had arrived at the house looking poised and sophisticated and breathtakingly beautiful, and he had suspected then and there that there wouldn't be a moment's peace from that time on. Lorie, he thought with slightly mixed emotions, was his unconventional daughter, the only one of the four who didn't give a hoot for what people thought of her and never followed the crowd in anything, from fashion to new dance steps. Lorie was an individualist, a rebel, a girl who had always done exactly what she pleased and would almost certainly keep on doing it no matter what the consequences.

No one could have been more surprised than Stuart when, four years ago, she'd turned down the idea of attending the college in nearby Whitewater and announced that she intended to go to the American University in Paris to learn "some lessons in life," as she'd put it, as well as in academics. At first he'd been dead set against the idea, worried that she was too young and impressionable to be on her own, so far away from her family and everything that was familiar to her. But Lorie—obstinate, uncompromising Lorie—had launched a campaign to convince him, and he'd ended up not only sending her to Paris, but buying her an entire new wardrobe of very expensive and, to his mind, not very practical clothes to take with her.

And now she was back with a diploma in journalism, and he had to admit he was proud of her for that. It was only natural that he, a newspaperman, should want one of his offspring to follow in his footsteps, and although Lorie could be infuriating and unpredictable, her untamed spirit and unique views on life could possibly make her into one hell of a writer. To his dismay, however, she'd turned down the idea of going to work at the *Chronicle* when he'd first presented it to her a few days after her return.

"We could use you, Lorie," he'd told her when he'd finally gotten a chance to speak to her alone, away from all the frantic preparations for Chris' wedding.

"As what?" his lovely, spoiled daughter had demanded, unimpressed. "Society editor?"

"No," Stuart had replied, ignoring the sarcasm in her voice. "We happen to have a very good one. But she could always use an assistant."

Lorie had smiled sweetly, but her sarcasm had remained. "I don't think she'd find me quite the type," she'd drawled.

"Honey," Stuart had urged, wanting earnestly to reach this girl and develop whatever talent lay within her, "whatever would interest you—we have a place for you."

Obviously having no intention of going along with the idea and refusing to be trapped into it, she had deftly managed to put an abrupt end to the conversation. "Let's just leave it open for now, shall we?" she'd said prettily, her wide eyes staring at him with daughterly contriteness. Her words had implied that she might be willing to discuss a job at another time, but something in Stuart told him not to hold his breath. Lorie was her own person, and what she did or didn't do would depend on her own desires. She had even said after that that she didn't know whether she'd be remaining in Genoa City, hinting that a larger city like New York or Chicago might prove a better setting for her special charms.

And then—Stuart shook his head, remembering— about a week ago, the night he had returned with Jen and Peg from the church party, Lorie had taken him aside and told him she'd changed her mind.

"I've been thinking, Dad . . ." she'd said, her beautiful face solemn and thoughtful.

"About what?" he'd asked her.

She'd smiled enchantingly. "After the wedding, I'd like to take you up on that visit to the newspaper. I'd like to look around and see what it's all about."

Stuart had naturally been delighted, but as he put away his shaving things he couldn't help wondering what had made her change her mind so soon. No new, more exciting spot had opened up at the paper, and to his knowledge she hadn't met a young man who might provide a reason for her deciding Genoa City wouldn't be such a bad place in which to settle down.

Oh, well, he thought, stepping out of the bathroom into the adjoining master bedroom, he should have known better than to think Lorie would do *anything* he expected her to do. And he'd better not count on too much happening even now that she seemed to be interested in a job. Now that the wedding was over, he'd remind her of her request and tell her to come on down to the paper and look around. And whatever she decided to do after that would, hopefully, turn out to be the right decision for everyone concerned.

Brad slumped listlessly at his desk in the *Chronicle* office, still feeling some of the effects of the twenty-four-hour flu that had kept him in bed for the past two days and had caused him to miss Stuart's daughter's wedding.

I doubt if my absence was even noticed, he reflected with the irony he sometimes found hard to control. And I know of one person, at least, who must have been delighted that I didn't show.

He leaned back and sighed. Why should it bug him so much that Jennifer Brooks didn't like him? He didn't need her favor. Stuart liked him, and since Stuart, not Jennifer, was his boss, that was really all that mattered. Except . . .

As so often happened these days, his mind turned to Leslie. Leslie was Jennifer's daughter, and he was sure her reluctance to allow him to call for her at home or even mention to anyone that they saw each other had a good deal to do with her mother's attitude. Again, it really shouldn't matter to him. He and Leslie were just friends—it wasn't as if he were courting her and wanted to make a good impression on her parents as well. But he *liked* Leslie, he liked her a hell of a lot, and he didn't want their friendship to cause any problems between her and her mother.

He wondered how Leslie had looked at the wedding in her long bridesmaid gown and a soft, velvet ribbon wound through her long, loose-falling hair.

I'll bet she looked like a million dollars, he mused, his mouth curving up in a smile. I'll bet people who knew her as that dowdy little Brooks girl who played the piano hardly even recognized her.

Bragging wasn't usually his style, but it was hard not to remind himself how far he'd brought Leslie in these past few months.

"Excuse me."

Startled by the presence of someone he hadn't heard come in, he looked up to see a staggeringly beautiful young woman standing over him, grinning down at him with the confidence of someone who knows she's devastatingly attractive to men and enjoys it to the hilt.

"Yes?" Brad asked, not sure he liked the way she

had sneaked up on him. He kept his voice polite but cool.

"I notice Mr. Brooks' door is closed." The girl looked at him apologetically from beneath heavily fringed lashes. "Is he in a meeting?"

"Not that I know of," Brad told her, still unsmiling and giving her no food whatsoever for what he was sure must be a gigantic ego. "Do you have an appointment?"

The girl grinned again and tossed her thick mane of glossy, sun-streaked hair. "I don't think I need one," she informed him importantly. "I'm his daughter."

Brad narrowed his dark eyes. Stuart's daughter. The one who'd recently returned from Paris. The one with the journalism degree whom he'd been hoping would go to work here at the *Chronicle,* but who, since she'd been home, had shown no interest whatsoever in so much as visiting the place. "Well," he said, a touch of sarcasm in his deep voice, "you finally got here." When the girl said nothing, merely widened her eyes and cocked her head quizzically, he added, frowning, "You *are* Lauralee Brooks?"

She brushed back her hair with a delicate, carefully manicured hand. "Yes, that's right."

"So . . . are you coming to work?" She didn't look as if she would last five minutes in the frantic world of a newspaper office, so frivolous and seductive did she appear in her disconcertingly short miniskirt and tight white sweater.

"No," she answered breezily, "just a visit."

Her cool assurance annoyed Brad and he couldn't keep from challenging cuttingly, "What's the matter? You afraid?"

Lorie looked at him in surprise. "Of what?" she asked with amused interest.

He set his jaw and fixed her with a cold, penetrating look. "That you can't cut it?"

Lorie's expression changed then, and the smugness on her face disappeared and was replaced by a glint of anger. "That's a very dumb thing to say!" she lashed out defensively.

"What other reason could there be? Or," Brad probed relentlessly, "is fun and games all you want out of life?"

He could tell she felt the sting. She lifted her head haughtily and the green eyes glared. "Who are you?" she demanded, her voice icy and irritated.

"Just someone who happens to respect your father one hell of a lot and hates seeing him put down by anyone, much less his own daughter."

Lorie took a deep, purposeful breath. "You're very impertinent," she exclaimed indignantly.

"Listen," Brad told her, his voice taking on a quiet intensity, "the man has waited four years for you to get your journalism degree. Spent Lord knows how much money . . . and for what?"

"I don't think it's any of your damned business!"

Brad smiled inwardly. He knew it wasn't any of his damned business, and he was enjoying making it his business immensely. For some reason he, who was usually such a perfect gentleman where women were concerned, suddenly felt like sticking a pin in this inflated little beauty queen. "What's wrong?" he asked her scornfully. "Don't men usually talk to you this way?" When he saw how she was struggling to maintain a semblance of composure, he went on, brutally pressing his advantage. "That's your problem, girl. You're too self-centered. Think about that."

He reached into his proof basket and pulled out a handful of galleys waiting to be read. "Now if you don't mind," he said, dismissing her without another glance, "I have work to finish."

Lorie said nothing to this, but he was aware of her eyes on him for a long moment before she finally turned and went back to Stuart's office, her dainty heels clicking purposefully on the shabby linoleum floor.

God, what a woman! he thought, when Stuart's door had closed behind her and he could drop his pretense of being busy. So stuck on herself you'd think she was the only woman in the world. Of course, he had to admit she was damned good-looking. Probably had men fawning over her day and night. She was one of those girls who just naturally attracted the opposite sex, and if his guess was correct, undoubtedly used them until she was tired of them, and then dropped them like old, worn-out toys.

I hope to God she doesn't decide to come to work here, he thought with real dread. Her posturing and conceit would drive him bats. Far better for her to go to New York and try to get a job on a women's magazine. Perhaps she could write those articles about how to lure men and make pets out of them.

He turned back to the galleys and willed himself to put Lauralee Brooks out of his mind. She wasn't worth wasting a thought on, much less diverting him from his work. He was deep in concentration when, some twenty minutes later, he heard Stuart's door open and the two of them come out. Brad did not look up as his boss ushered his daughter up to his desk. It was not until Stuart said eagerly, "I don't think you two have met, have you?" that Brad raised his head and met Lorie's eyes.

"No," she told her father, a statement that Brad had to grudgingly admit was true in one sense. He hadn't told her *his* name.

Stuart smiled and made the introduction. "Lorie, my right-hand man, Brad Eliot. Brad, I'd like you to meet my daughter, Lauralee."

"Lauralee," Brad replied with a polite smile.

"Hello," she answered back, a friendly smile on her beautiful face.

Isn't there any honesty in her at all? Brad wondered, hoping she'd get out of here now that her duty to her father was over. He didn't like feeling so antagonistic toward one of Stuart's daughters, but this vainglorious and somehow disturbing young woman was one person he'd just as soon not see again.

It was with a great deal of effort that he managed to restrain a groan when, in the next moment, Stuart announced with fatherly pride, "And, Brad, as of tomorrow morning Lorie's going to be working with us."

4

Might as well resign myself to having her around, he decided the next morning, watching her bent over her desk, her red lips pursed seductively as she worked on the list of ideas for her column she planned to present to her father a little later. She'd decided she wanted to use the photographic knowledge she'd acquired in Paris as well as her writing talent, Stuart had told Brad after his talk with his daughter yesterday. She wanted to be sort of an inquiring photographer, go out on the street and ask people how they felt about pertinent issues and take pictures of them to run alongside their quotes.

"After all, that's the way Jackie Kennedy got started," she'd informed her father by way of convincing him that a column of her own was what she needed to start off her journalistic career with a bang.

Stuart would have agreed to almost anything to have her working there, Brad knew. He'd even promised to run a short article on Lorie herself, introducing her to the readers and thereby hopefully stirring up interest in this new *Chronicle* feature. Brad had recently written a piece on Leslie, who was in Chicago at the moment rehearsing with the Mid-America Symphony, and Lorie had told Stuart she'd thought it was so good she'd like Brad to write hers as well.

Stuart had thought the idea showed excellent thinking on Lorie's part, but Brad wasn't so sure there wasn't something more than a desire to herald the new column behind it. An article on Les followed so quickly

29

by an article on Lorie? It seemed to him that Stuart
Brooks' second daughter was determined not to let
the first one take the wind out of her sails. She, who
had always been the dazzler of the family, had returned
from Paris to find her position threatened if not completely overshadowed by the one sister she'd never
dreamed would prove to be competition—and she was
doing everything she could to make her own presence
felt as flashily as possible.

Oh, well, he thought as he turned back to the piece
he was writing on nursing homes in Genoa City. Guess
I should mind my own business and stop worrying
about what's in that pretty head of Lorie Brooks'. Perhaps he was all wrong about her anyway. Maybe under
all that gloss and silly female behavior she actually had
the brains and talent Stuart boasted of. He had to admit she looked very engrossed in her work just now. She
was wearing a conservative pantsuit that made her seem
more businesslike than she had seemed yesterday in that
preposterous miniskirt. And at the moment, her dis-
concerting mop of hair was held demurely in place by
a wide silk scarf. If that damn perfume of hers weren't
wafting across the room and filling his nostrils so maddeningly, he could almost think of her as just another
Chronicle employee.

"Mr. Eliot?" He'd been working on his piece for
some time when her voice, soft and suspiciously polite,
broke through his thoughts. He looked up to see her
standing beside his desk, looking at him speculatively.

"Yes?" He instinctively put up his defenses. Did
she want something legitimate, or was she planning to
try her womanly wiles on him again and test his reaction?

"Did Dad talk to you about the story about me?"
She seemed hesitant, uncertain as to how she should
handle this.

"Yes," he told her without enthusiasm. "He talked
to me about it."

She smiled and some of her old assurance came

through. "Would you like to interview me after you finish with what you're doing?"

Brad sighed inwardly. He should have known. A couple of hours at work and she was pushing him for that damned interview! He guessed she wanted it run quickly, lest Leslie have some new triumph and get the edge on her again.

"Why?" he asked boldly, giving her a disdainful glare. "Are you jealous of Leslie?"

Lorie was obviously thrown, but she managed to keep her composure. "Why ever would you think a thing like that?" she asked, looking very innocent and put out.

Brad eyed her evenly. "You're very competitive, Lorie. And your sister's doing something rather spectacular."

She smiled. "Yes, big sister is surprising us all."

"Not all," he corrected. "Just you."

Lorie shrugged, as if this particular vein of conversation had no interest for her. "She has her thing. I have mine."

He frowned. "The column, you mean?" If he was any judge of Lorie Brooks, she wasn't going to be satisfied with doing a couple of local interviews every day.

"Oh," she replied with a small laugh, "I assure you I have much more in mind than just a column for a small-town paper."

"You have something better in mind?"

"Oh, yes," she insisted airily.

"A secret?"

"Not to you. If you're interested."

He leaned back in his chair and studied her for a long moment. "Might be another clue to your character," he observed dryly.

"You'd like one?" Lorie's voice suddenly took on a teasing tone.

"I always like to understand the people around me," he replied coolly.

"And you haven't figured me out yet?"

"Not quite."

The slanted green eyes mocked him. "My secret would help you out," she said in a singsong, like a child who knows where the candy is hidden and isn't sure she wants to tell.

"Are you telling?" he asked irritably. "Or just playing games?"

She bit her lip and looked at him, as if trying to decide whether to tell him or keep him in suspense a little longer. Finally, she decided to go ahead. "I'm writing a book," she announced, a ring of triumph in her voice.

Brad's eyebrows shot up. "Oh?"

"You're the first person I've told."

"I'll keep it to myself," he assured her drolly.

She responded with a droll rejoinder of her own. "I understand you're very good at keeping things to yourself," she said smiling, her voice dripping with a nuance he could not fail to catch.

"I'd like to read your book sometime," he remarked, letting it pass in a determined effort not to let her get to him. "Something to do with you?" And here his *voice* contained a certain nuance, "Your adventures in Europe?"

"What else?" Lorie replied.

He was amused by her bald confidence. He had seen it before, in others—and it was usually entirely unmerited. "Lots of youngsters in journalism think they can write the great American novel," he scoffed.

If she felt put down, she didn't show it. "This is one who'll really do it," she said quietly.

"That the way you think you'll top Leslie?"

She laughed at that. "I'm not worried about Leslie, Mr. Eliot," she replied coolly. When he offered no rejoinder, she lifted her hands in a gesture of dismissal. "Well . . . when you're ready to begin that story on me . . ." She turned and took a step back toward her own desk.

"Since you're such a good writer," Brad called after her, "I'll let you write it yourself."

She turned and looked at him in surprise.

"It'll be a good exercise on who and what you think you are."

Far better *you* should do it, he reflected as, after deliberating for a moment, she tossed him a self-satisfied smile and walked, hips swinging, back to her desk. I might reveal what you *really* are.

The Genoa City lights should be coming into view any minute now, Leslie reflected as she leaned across her big, comfortable airplane seat to search through the blackness outside the window for a sign that they'd be landing soon.

She knew nobody would be at the airport to meet her; the family wasn't expecting her home until tomorrow. But, she thought, leaning back in her seat, her eyes growing distant as she sank into a lovely reverie, the sooner I get back, the sooner I'll see . . . him.

She'd thought about Brad so often during the short time she'd been in Chicago for the symphony rehearsals. As usual, it had been he who had calmed her nerves before she'd left and sent her off to Maestro Fautsch with the confidence that was flagging so frighteningly before she'd called and asked to see him.

"You're a deeply sensitive woman, Leslie," he'd told her in answer to her agonized confession of doubts and fears. "It's what makes you the exceptional artist you are." He had smiled reassuringly. "Experience will give you the confidence you need to control these doubts."

"You make it sound so easy," she'd replied shakily, not sure she believed it entirely.

"No, never easy," he'd countered quickly. "An artist's self-confidence is often as difficult to acquire as his technique. But with time, it'll come easier. And when you're up there, in front of that orchestra, you'll be lost in your music. Your talent will be in complete control. You'll be in the world you know best."

Of course he'd been right. For all her anxieties, Leslie *had* been in control, so much so Maestro Fautsch had told her he wanted her to play several selections by herself when the tour began, in addition to playing with the orchestra. "You're going to be the newest star in our world, my dear child," he'd promised her, his kindly old wizened face looking at her with genuine affection. "I am going to be very proud of my young protégée."

She could hardly wait to tell Brad the news. She could imagine how his face would break into that beautiful smile of his and how his eyes would shine with happiness for her.

Brad Eliot. His very name made her tingle. He had done so much for her; she owed him so much. How she longed to tell him what he meant to her, what he would always mean to her! But of course she couldn't open up her heart to him so utterly. Even Lorie, who probably knew more about men than anyone Leslie had ever known, had advised her to keep her cool where Brad was concerned if she didn't want to scare him away.

"Telling Brad how you feel about him is the worst thing you could do," Lorie had insisted the night when, just before leaving for Chicago, Leslie had expressed an urgent desire to stop holding it all in and tell the man exactly how she felt. "Men want excitement and intrigue. They enjoy a challenge."

"Play games?" Leslie had asked, eyeing her sister doubtfully.

"That's the greatest game of all, big sister," Lorie had replied with a knowing wink. "The one between a man and a woman."

Leslie had become thoughtful. Imagine playing games with Brad! Brad . . . who was so incredibly honest with her.

"I wouldn't know how to start," she'd told her sister, shaking her head firmly.

Lorie had smiled tolerantly and taken on the superior air of one knew exactly how such things worked. "The first thing you ought to do is make Brad think you have other men in your life," she'd insisted.

"Give him a sense of competition. If you make it too easy for a man, he loses interest."

Sitting in the cabin of the airplane, soaring through a darkened sky, Leslie had to admit she was probably right. She didn't have much experience with men herself, but she'd heard plenty of tales of woe about girls who lost their men because they'd thrown themselves at them.

I'll just keep my feelings to myself, she decided resignedly. And maybe someday *he'll* make a move in *my* direction.

She would call him to tell him about the rehearsals, though, she resolved. Calling a man to tell him about her work couldn't be considered throwing herself at him—particularly since the man in question was responsible for her success in that work.

She looked at her watch. Twelve-fifteen. It was too late to call him tonight. She'd have to wait and try to catch him at the office tomorrow. Maybe she'd even suggest taking him to dinner tomorrow night by way of thanking him for all his help. Then she could tell him everything—all about Maestro Fautsch, her solos, and the way the orchestra had applauded her when she'd finished the Chopin number this morning.

She was sure Lorie wouldn't approve of her suggesting the dinner. But she'd be very careful not to say anything personal to him, not to make him feel she considered the evening a date. They'd just be two friends—like they'd always been—meeting at Pierre's and talking about music and philosophy and how very wonderful life could be.

Suddenly the FASTEN SEAT BELTS light flashed on, and Leslie strained toward the window to see a mass of lights coming into view. "Ladies and gentlemen," the flight attendant's voice announced over the loudspeaker, "were are preparing for our landing in Genoa City. Please observe the seat-belt and no-smoking signs and put your seat backs in an upright position."

Leslie felt a wave of pleasure as she felt the plane losing altitude and finally touch ground on the airport runway. What she'd just left in Chicago was very important to her, but there was something here in Genoa City that she felt pulling her more and more every day.

5

By the time she reached him the next day, it was too late. She called the paper twice in the morning, and both times he was out on assignment. Once, a man had answered Brad's phone and taken a message for him to call her back. And the second time, Les had talked to Lorie, who had promised she'd have him call the minute he walked in the door.

But he didn't get back to her until afternoon, and when she suggested the dinner she'd been thinking about since last night, he had to decline.

"Sorry, Les," he said, sounding truly apologetic. "I just made plans for tonight."

Leslie was so disappointed she couldn't speak for a moment, merely stood in the second-floor hallway holding the phone and biting her lower lip in frustration.

"Fact is," Brad went on, his voice sounding oddly ironic, "I lost a bet to your cagey sister Lorie, and I have to pay off with dinner."

Lorie? Les was so stunned that she nearly dropped the phone. Why would Lorie be going to dinner with Brad? Especially tonight, when she *knew* Leslie had her heart set on seeing him. When Les had arrived home from the airport last night, Lorie had been awake, and they'd talked then about Les' success and how much she wanted to share it with Brad. And when she'd called the office today, Lorie had known it was to ask him to dinner.

"How about tomorrow night?" Brad's voice broke

37

through her whirling thoughts. "I want to hear all about Chicago."

Leslie stared, unseeing, into space. "Sure," she answered dully.

"I'll call about this time. Take care, Les."

The phone clicked off. Slowly, Leslie replaced the receiver and stood motionlessly for what must have been several minutes. She couldn't believe it. Lorie, moving in on her ground. Lorie, whom she'd confided in and come to trust so completely these past few weeks.

She replayed her conversation with Brad in her head. He'd said something about having to pay off a bet. What could he have meant by that? What kind of a bet would be paid off with dinner—and who's idea was it anyway?

She stewed over it the rest of the afternoon. By the time Lorie got home from work she was consumed with anger, and her sister had scarcely removed her coat and scarf before she had flown down the stairs and demanded an explanation.

"Just what are you trying to do, Lorie?" she exploded, her whole face contorted with fury. She felt as if she were fighting for her very life.

"Trying to do?" Lorie repeated, her eyes widening in bewilderment. "What on earth are you talking about?"

"Why?" Leslie shouted, knowing full well she was faking that damned innocence. God, how she hated her at this moment!

Lorie, as always, remained unperturbed. "I don't get you," she said with an indifferent shrug, and turning away, she proceeded to start up the stairs.

"Don't play games with me, Lorie," Leslie snapped, grabbing her arm and whirling her around with a forcefulness that made Lorie eye her, for the first time, with real concern.

"You're really throwing me, Les," she said, still all bewilderment and injured pride. "How about laying it out?"

Leslie glared at her and swallowed hard. Lorie was making it as difficult as possible for her and it took a moment for her to muster up the courage to reveal her devastating agony. "How'd you maneuver things so Brad would take you out to dinner tonight?" she cried at last.

As soon as the accusing words were out, Lorie's delicate face broke into a relieved smile. "Oh, that . . ." she replied lightly, as if she'd expected something much more serious. She shrugged, as if to dismiss it.

"I told you last night I was going to ask Brad to have dinner with *me*."

"Les, I'm sorry!" Lorie put her hands up to her face in deep agitation. "You did tell me, but it completely slipped my mind!"

"How could it?" Leslie's voice was cold.

"Honey . . . the whole thing was so ridiculous."

"Was it?" Leslie glared at her, unmoved by her pretty cajoling.

"Brad was positive I wouldn't have my column ready by deadline. He bet me a dinner I couldn't do it."

"He bet *you?*" For the first time since her conversation with Brad, Leslie began to feel uncertain. Was it possible Lorie *wasn't* to blame?

"Typical male chauvinism," Lorie answered, raising her eyes to the heavens wearily. "I couldn't let him get away with a challenge like that."

"So," Leslie said slowly, the meaning of her words sinking in and understanding how such a thing could have happened, "you won the bet."

Lorie flashed a triumphant smile. "I *knew* I'd finish in time." Then her green eyes narrowed and she addressed her sister scornfully. "Really, Les, I know you think he's great, but he can be so overbearing, so sure of himself. The kind of man who infuriates me." As Leslie stared at her in silence, still trying to decide whether she was telling the truth, she went on with great earnestness. "Look, Les, I couldn't care less about going out with him. The high and mighty Mr.

Eliot's far from my cup of tea." She turned and started to walk briskly toward the living room. "I'm going to call him right now and break the date," she called back over her shoulder. "Then you can make plans with him."

"No!" Leslie cried, catching up with her frantically. "Don't do that. He might think I'm jealous."

Lorie stopped before reaching the phone and turned back to her, her beautiful face filled with dismay. "I feel terrible about it," she insisted, her eyes looking into Leslie's appealingly. "Please let me call him, Les."

"No," Leslie said firmly. She felt silly and foolish. "I shouldn't have gotten so upset."

"You didn't understand." The younger girl smiled at her reassuringly.

"I was silly."

"I feel awful—your thinking I was trying to pull something on you." Lorie dropped her eyes as if the whole thing were extremely painful to her. The expression on her face caused Les to feel uncomfortably guilty.

"I'm sorry, Lorie," she said quickly. "I should've known you wouldn't do anything to hurt me."

Lorie looked at her uncertainly. "I'd still like to break the date," she told her.

"No, you can't do that." Les was feeling worse and worse.

"Why not? I made my point by winning the bet."

Leslie smiled, and the old warmth came back into her voice. "You should get the payoff, too." Then a new thought entered her head and she added eagerly, "I'd like you to get to know him better, anyway."

To that, Lorie shook her head and groaned. "I see enough of him at the office," she declared caustically.

"Maybe in a social setting you'll get to like him more." Leslie's manner became more urgent. "I really *do* want you to like him, Lorie."

Lorie was thoughtful for a moment, and then she

broke into a warm, sisterly smile. "Well, I don't know about that," she said to Les. "But as long as you insist I keep this date, I'd better run up and get dressed."

Leslie smiled back. "Sure. Go ahead."

She watched her as she bounced up the stairs, already tearing at her clothes in what Les knew was an unusual effort to be ready on time. Then she eased herself in a chair in the steadily darkening living room and bit her thumb, hard, to keep from crying.

The restaurant had cleared out considerably by the time Sally Rolland had placed their after-dinner coffee in front of them. It had been a long, leisurely meal, and though the conversation had been spiked with plenty of barbs tossed out by both of them, Lorie was enjoying her dinner with Brad Eliot thoroughly.

This guy is a real man, she thought admiringly as she looked across the table at his strong, masculine face. I'm not sure how he feels about me at this point. He probably still thinks I'm a frivolous little nothing. Her lips formed a thin, determined smile. But that's all right. He's a challenge, and I like challenges. No matter what he thinks now, one of these days he'll realize that I'm an intelligent, clever, modern woman. *A woman,* not a girl. Full of warmth and passion and fire. That's what a man like Brad Eliot needs. Passion and fire. Not a simpering little milkmaid like big sister Les.

The thought of Leslie made her squirm inwardly. That confrontation this evening hadn't been easy to deal with. Les had shown more spunk than she'd thought her capable of when she suspected Lorie had stolen Brad from under her nose.

Whew! Lorie thought with relief. It took everything I had to get her off my back and convince her that Brad was the guilty one.

Her mind darted back to this afternoon, when Brad had returned to the office after almost a whole day's absence and she had hit upon the idea of maneuvering him into this little dinner date. She'd just finished her column when he arrived, but on impulse she'd covered it with a sheet of blank paper just before he walked by her desk and asked how she was doing.

"No way are you going to finish that column in time for today's edition," he'd said reprovingly, as she stared at the blank page and pretended to rack her brain for something clever to write on it.

"Got a late start," Lorie had said with feigned consternation. "But I'll finish."

Brad had looked at his watch. "You've got exactly one hour." Lorie had looked up at him then, and her eyes shone mischievously. "What do you bet I make it?" she challenged.

Brad had shrugged. "You name it."

"Dinner tonight if I do?"

He'd smiled. "You're on."

They'd shaken on it, and as soon as Brad had gone to his own desk, Lorie had pulled out the completed column and taken it over to him.

Too bad, big sister, she'd thought flippantly, knowing how outraged Leslie would be if she knew. But you know what they say about love and war.

Now the dinner was over and Lorie searched for a way to make the evening last. If what she suspected about Brad's opinion of her was accurate, he'd consider his obligation ended with the coffee and have no desire to linger further with her.

"Do you like living upstairs?" she asked him, trying to put the conversation on a "safe" level so at least the evening wouldn't end with fireworks.

"It's comfortable," Brad replied. He poured some cream in his coffee and stirred it with his spoon.

"Now that I'm working, I'm thinking of getting a place of my own."

He showed no particular interest. "Plenty of apartments in town," he remarked coolly.

"What's it like here?" Lorie was looking at him brightly, trying hard to draw him out.

He shook his head. "Don't think it's your style."

"I'd like to see your room. So I could decide for myself." Her voice was very light, very casual. Brad looked at her with an amused glint in his eyes. She could tell he knew she was up to something. "Might be just what I'm looking for," she went on ingenuously.

He studied her thoughtfully for a moment. Then he rose from his seat and moved to pull her chair back from the table. "All right," he said, a little to her surprise, "I'll show you."

Together they walked toward the stairs that led from the restaurant to the floor above. Brad led the way as they went up, and when they reached his room, he opened the door and flicked on the overhead light switch.

As he stood aside, Lorie stepped in and looked around curiously. The tinyness of the room, the drabness, the old, worn-out furniture surprised her, but she said nothing.

"I told you," Brad said, as if reading her mind.

Lorie nodded. "You told me."

"Suits my needs," he said.

She flashed a provocative smile. "Man of simple tastes."

Her nuance was not lost on him. "On occasion," he admitted evenly.

Lorie strolled through the room, touching the furniture and casting an interested eye over his personal things that lay on the dresser and end table. Brush and comb. Jewelry box. Cigarette lighter. The sort of things you might find in any man's bedroom. Nothing at all that gave so much as a clue as to who this particular man really was. No photographs of parents or girl friends or family of any kind. No letters with out-of-town postmarks, no mementos of things past and held dear.

"I don't understand a man like you living in one room over a restaurant," she remarked thoughtfully, running her hand over the back of the worn-out easy chair.

"That's the only thing you don't understand about me?" Brad asked, amused.

Lorie looked up at him and their eyes met. "There are lots of things I'd like to understand better," she said, her voice becoming unusually husky.

He held her glance. "Why?"

"Didn't we agree we both like to know what makes people tick?"

He stepped toward her and cupped her chin—a little tighter than necessary—in his strong, firm hand. His eyes bored into her face. "What makes you tick, Lorie?"

She smiled and tossed her unruly mane of hair. "Part of the fun will be finding out for yourself."

He dropped his hand, and his eyes narrowed. "I have an idea I've got a line on you already," he informed her.

"Tell me." She was finding his nearness increasingly exciting. She had to hold herself in tight to keep from reaching out and touching his face.

"You might not like to hear."

Lorie had to scoff at that. Did he think she was Leslie? "I told you once before," she reminded him, "I don't scare easily."

Brad chuckled. "Supreme self-confidence."

"Isn't that good?" She widened her eyes and gave him her innocent look.

"It can be carried too far."

Lorie dropped into the easy chair and stretched her long, shapely legs out before her. "You think I have?" she asked, laying her head back and looking up at him lazily.

"You're selfish," Brad told her with a tolerant, amused smile. "And self-centered."

Lorie heaved an exaggerated sigh. "Guilty on both counts," she agreed genially.

"Beautiful . . . provocative . . ."

"That's better." She gave a slow smile.

He studied the legs that, thanks to her red miniskirt, were uncovered all the way to her thighs. "I thought miniskirts were old-fashioned," he observed dryly, his expression maddeningly enigmatic.

"I don't follow the crowd."

Brad nodded, as if it were the answer he'd expected. "You do your own thing."

Lorie raised her head and looked straight into his eyes. The indisputable challenge she saw there made her tingle, and her toes curled involuntarily in her tight-fitting boots. "Always," she told him meaningfully.

The hypnotic moment held for a moment, and then he turned away with a scornful little laugh. "The sophisticated lady," he said sardonically. Then, unexpectedly, he turned back and addressed her seriously. "Know what I think you are, Lorie?"

She found it difficult to be serious in return. "Love to know what's on your mind," she said pertly.

"You're a spoiled little girl playing grown-up games."

At that, Lorie rose languidly from the chair, and with utter self-assurance moved so close to him that her face was very nearly touching his. "I'd like to play games with you," she said mockingly, her voice low and seductive. "Might be fun to spoil you." Boldly, she put one cool hand behind his neck and pulled his head down until their lips met. It was a brief, unimpassioned kiss, but after it was over, they remained standing close together, their eyes locked, Brad looking at her intently as if trying to decide what to do.

"I want to know you a lot better, Brad Eliot," Lorie declared. Her lips parted and her eyes held a definite invitation.

It took no more than a second for Brad to make his decision. With a rough, deliberate gesture, he pulled her tight into his arms and kissed her hard, almost brutally, on her soft, yielding lips.

But it was over almost as quickly as it had begun. Suddenly, exasperatingly, she found herself being pushed away, and Brad regarding her with scornful distaste. "Score one for you, Lorie Brooks," he spat disdainfully. And then, turning maddeningly polite, he asked, "Shall I drive you home or would you rather I call a cab?"

6

The Brooks household was in a stir. Time was rushing on with dizzying speed, and tomorrow Leslie was to go to Chicago again—only this time she wasn't going there to rehearse. The moment they'd all been waiting for was upon them. Leslie Brooks was going to make her first public appearance as soloist with the Mid-America Symphony Orchestra.

Naturally, Stuart and Jennifer planned to be in the audience to witness their daughter's thrilling debut. And an excited Peggy had talked them into letting her skip school for a day so she could be there, too, to cheer her sister on. Unfortunately, Chris' husband, Snapper, couldn't get off duty at the hospital, and although Chris wanted badly to go, she didn't feel she should leave her husband overnight so soon after their marriage, and she had to offer her sorrowful apologies.

Lorie, to the family's dismay, wasn't going to be there either. Looking convincingly devastated, she had told Les she simply couldn't let her column go for a day this soon in the game.

"You do understand, don't you?" she'd asked beseechingly, her eyes wide and earnest. "If I shirked my duty when I've only just begun, everybody would say I only got the job because I'm the boss's daughter, and I'm not serious about my work."

"It's all right, honey," Les had assured her, squeezing her hand affectionately. "I know your column comes first."

There was one other person Les had hoped would be there, but he, too, had had to disappoint her in her most glorious hour. Leslie had stopped by the newspaper office the day she'd bought the gown she intended to wear, and she'd asked Brad a little shyly if he could possibly take some time off work to see the result of all his guidance and encouragement.

"If I knew you were in the audience, I'd feel so much less anxious," she'd confessed, her eyes holding a wistful appeal.

Brad had given her a warm smile, but he shook his head. "I think you ought to let just your parents share that glory with you. Let them have Chicago," he'd urged when Les' face had dropped. "I'll catch you when you appear in Detroit."

Leslie had managed to muster a small smile. No use making it any more difficult for him. "If that's the way you want it," she told him resignedly.

"Definitely Detroit," Brad had promised. "I'd much rather show you that town than Chicago."

Now, standing over the ironing board, pressing the things she'd need to take with her, she heaved a long, unhappy sigh. Here she was, hours away from making the dream of her life come true, on the way—if what Maestro Fautsch had predicted were true—to a brilliant future in the concert world, and she felt only a sense of being let down. She knew she shouldn't really have expected Brad to come. They were friends, good friends, but he had other things to do with his life than trail around catching her concerts miles away from Genoa City.

But the *first* one! She shook her head in frustration. If it turned out to be a success, a great deal of the credit would be his. And he wouldn't be there to share in it.

She began to imagine what it would be like if he *could* be there; if, for instance, he surprised her and turned up backstage afterwards unexpectedly. He'd take her for a midnight supper, perhaps, and they'd celebrate and maybe drink a toast to her career. And,

Leslie reflected, her breath quickening a little, her knees beginning to feel weak, that would be the moment in which she would finally be able to tell him what was in her heart, the moment in which she would thank him for all he'd done for her and tell him—yes, *tell him* at last—how deeply she'd come to love him.

Yes, Leslie thought, staring blankly at the silk blouse stretched out on the ironing board, that would be the moment for her long-awaited confession.

"Like your gown," Lorie announced, swinging into the room they shared and bringing Leslie back to reality with an abrupt jolt. "It'll be very effective on stage."

"Thanks." Leslie, feeling almost as if her sister could hear the thoughts she had interrupted, and blushing slightly at the idea, turned her attention quickly to the blouse.

Lorie's eyes, which never missed anything, went to the gigantic poster advertising the concert that leaned against the wall next to Les' bed. Wordlessly, she took in the spectacularly glamorous photograph and the words LESLIE BROOKS, SOLOIST, printed across the bottom in big, bold letters.

"Impressive," she mused almost to herself, wrinkling her brow thoughtfully.

Leslie gave a weak smile. The poster embarrassed her. It was so huge! So imposing! And she was so ordinary and insignificant. "I just hope I can live up to the maestro's expectations," she replied apprehensively.

"Sorry I can't be in Chicago for your big moment," Lorie remarked, turning away and rummaging through her scarf drawer with great concentration.

"I'm sorry, too."

There was a moment of silence as both girls busied themselves and then Lorie said offhandedly, "Brad'll be there, of course."

Leslie's face clouded. "Afraid not."

"Why not? Dad would have let him off." There was an underlying note of cynicism in Lorie's voice.

"I talked to Brad about it," Leslie said, knowing

how strange it must seem that the man she loved would miss such an important event. "But he thinks the night should be just for Mom and Dad."

Lorie pulled the scarf she was looking for out of the drawer and, standing before the mirror, experimented with ways of tying it around her neck. "The folks wouldn't mind sharing it with him," she argued.

Leslie shook her head sadly. "He'd rather catch the concert in Detroit. I gather he doesn't like Chicago so much."

Lorie let the scarf drop and she looked at Leslie, hard, through the mirror. "Did he say why?" she asked, frowning.

"No. But he definitely won't go to Chicago."

The younger girl turned around to face her sister squarely. "Not very generous of him," she observed disapprovingly. "I'm sure you made it plain you want him."

The inference in her voice nettled Les. "He must have his own very good reasons," she said snappishly. Then, realizing how childish her retort must have seemed, she looked up and begged miserably, "Look, let's not talk about it anymore, O.K.?"

She finished the sleeve she was working on and pulled the blouse off the ironing board. As she went to the closet for a hanger, she noted that Lorie was deep in thought, her eyes holding a faraway look, but glittering keenly.

Chicago. Brad Eliot. Lorie mulled over the two names in her ever-active mind. Was there some connection between them?

Sitting at her dressing table, carefully stroking bright red polish on her long, tapered nails, her mind went back to that conversation with Leslie in which she'd tried in her foolish, loyal way to explain why Brad would be missing the concert.

"He definitely won't go to Chicago." Those were almost Leslie's exact words. Lorie weighed them carefully. It couldn't have been because he didn't want to attend the concert. For all that he had kissed her, Lorie, in his room that night when she'd won the bet, she knew that he had a deep fondness for her sister and a genuine interest in her career. And, as she'd told Les, Dad would definitely have let him off if he'd asked to go to Chicago to hear her play.

"He'd rather catch the concert in Detroit." Les had said that, too. So, obviously, it was the city he wanted to avoid tomorrow night, not the concert or missing work. Lorie's mouth pursed thoughtfully. Was Chicago the place the man had come from—had *run* from? Was that the city that held the key that would unlock the past and rip the mask off the elusive, mysterious Brad Eliot?

Practically since the day they'd met, Lorie had persistently tried to learn the truth about this man she found so intriguing and exciting. She'd questioned everyone who knew him—her father; Les; even Jennifer, who didn't like him—in the hope that in sifting through all they knew about him there would be one small clue they'd missed that would reveal something, some tiny little deatil, about his background. And when that tack had failed, she had turned to Brad himself, cajoling him at times, baiting him at others, trying determinedly to catch him off guard and break through that damned barrier he'd built around himself.

Once she'd even tried to trick him into thinking she *knew* something about his past.

"Tell me about your wife," she'd said casually, thinking perhaps a straight statement of fact would throw him and cause him to give himself away.

But, managing, as always, to stay one step ahead of her, Brad had not even looked up from the galleys he'd been reading. "She's a head taller than I am," he'd said dryly. "And had a moustache, last I saw her."

And Lorie had had to admit defeat. Again.

Oh, well, she reflected, blowing her nails dry and reaching gingerly for the manila envelope she'd placed on the dressing table, there was plenty of time. She wasn't one to give up easily, and she was sure that eventually she'd either wear Brad down or her own ingenuity would ferret something out. Maybe, she speculated optimistically, she'd even glean a thing or two tonight. When she got to his room at Pierre's.

Wouldn't Leslie have a fit if she knew I was sneaking off from her pre-debut party to see Brad Eliot? she thought with amusement as she took a final critical glance at herself in the mirror and fluffed her hair with her hand. She'd told the family she had to do some interviews this evening, and sorry as she was not to be in on all the toasts and good wishes for Les, she insisted she simply couldn't postpone them.

The truth was she'd told Brad she wanted to drop her book by for him to take a look at tonight. Ever since she'd mentioned she'd been writing it that day in the office, he'd made occasional disparaging and cynical remarks. And this morning he'd told her quite baldly that her column, though very good, was no proof at all that she could write, since all she did was quote other people in it.

"You said you started a book in Europe," he'd reminded her, his look steady and challenging.

"I did," she'd answered levelly, meeting his eyes.

He'd studied her, almost as if he didn't believe her. Then he'd made an unexpected request. "I'd like to read it—see what you really can do." When she'd hesitated, not sure she was ready for anyone to take a look at it, he'd urged with wry skepticism, "Remember—you're the girl who's not afraid of anything."

Lorie had thrown her shoulders back defensively. "I'm not afraid. The writing's good."

Brad, still not hiding his doubts, had said something to the effect that he wouldn't believe it until he saw it for himself, and of course Lorie couldn't refuse a challenge like that. She'd informed him he'd be seeing her and her book later; she'd presented her little white lie to the family, and now she was all primed and ready to pay her second visit to Brad Eliot's modest little abode.

When he didn't answer her knock, she thought

for an angry moment he'd stood her up, but upon trying the door, she found it unlocked, and when she
walked brazenly inside, she heard the sound of the
shower running in the bathroom. Satisfied that he was
there, she closed the door behind her and deliberated
as to whether she should walk right in and pull the
shower curtain back. That would certainly give him a
little jolt, she thought with a mischievous grin, but on
second thought she decided she liked the idea of being
here without his knowing it even better. It was almost
as if she'd somehow stumbled upon the secret door that
led to his own private world.

For a second time her eyes searched the room for
some revealing picture or memento of his past, but, as
was the case the first time she'd been here, the table
and dresser were devoid of anything meaningful whatsoever. Totally unconcerned as to what would happen
should he walk out of the bathroom just now, she
pulled open a couple of drawers and peered inside. One
held underwear, the other shirts. All with labels from
Genoa City stores.

She spotted his billfold lying atop his chest of
drawers and she stared at it thoughtfully. She wasn't interested in how much money he had, but perhaps the
billfold contained a driver's license. That would at
least reveal where Brad Eliot was born.

It turned out that there was no driver's license inside, but Lorie's persistent probing fingers found a
folded piece of paper stuck in one of the compartments
and she pulled it out to examine it. It was a piece of
newswire copy, and the first thing that caught her eye
was the picture at the top of Brad himself. Knowing instinctively that she was on to something, she cast a furtive look in the direction of the bathroom, and satisfied
that the shower was still going strong, she smoothed out
the page and flopped herself into his easy chair while
she read the contents with mounting excitement.

A Chicago neurosurgeon and psychiatrist per-
ished in the flaming wreckage of the convertible

he was driving early this afternoon when he lost control on a slippery curve of U.S. Highway 10, fifteen miles west of Akron, Ohio. The victim was identified as Dr. Bradley Eliot, a staff surgeon of Northwestern Memorial Hospital in Chicago. State police said witnesses to the accident reported the car attempted to take a curve at high speed when it skidded, crashed through a guardrail, and ran off a thirty-foot embankment before bursting into flames. Attempts to rescue the single occupant were prevented by the intense heat of the flames and a gas-tank explosion. The coroner's office stated identification of the body was almost impossible due to the extent of injuries. Ownership of the car was determined through Illinois license plates. A close friend of Dr. Eliot, Miss Barbara Anderson, a registered nurse and part-time Chicago model, identified the body from the person belongings found near the scene of the crash. Associates of Northwestern Hospital told authorities that Dr. Eliot had left the hospital earlier today but had made no mention of leaving the city. Hospital personnel said that Dr. Eliot had several operations scheduled for the following day. Dr. Bradley Eliot was a graduate of Northwestern University and Northwestern Medical School. He had completed his residency in neurology at Northwestern Hospital before transferring to St. Elizabeth's Hospital, Washington, D.C. for a residency in psychiatry. He returned to practice in Chicago as a member of the Northwestern Hospital staff earlier this year. Dr. Eliot was the only child of Dr. and Mrs. James Eliot of Quincy, Illinois. The body is being returned to Quincy for services and burial.

Lorie stared at the paper a long time after she'd finished reading the article. *So.* Brad's secret was out at last. He was a doctor—a psychiatrist and neurosurgeon. She laughed a little as the pieces fell into place. No wonder he'd been able to work such miracles with Leslie! The man was a professional.

But why, she wondered, was he carrying around a

notice of his own death? Obviously, there had been some mistake made in Akron when Barbara Anderson —whoever she was—had identified the body. Lorie supposed that was understandable, considering how badly the body had been burned and maimed, according to the account. But why would he be holding on to such a ghoulish piece of misinformation? For laughs? No, surely not. Brad Eliot was many irritating things, but he was not a man with a sick sense of humor.

Could it be . . . Uh-uh. Her mind dismissed the thought, and then, unable to let it go completely, seized on it again. Could it be possible that Brad had never bothered to correct the error? That he was living the life of a mystery man here in Genoa City because he wanted everyone in Chicago to think he was actually dead?

She couldn't really imagine him doing such a thing. What about his parents? His friends? His patients, who depended on him? Was he so cruel he would actually let them think he was dead when he was alive?

Although she'd stumbled upon some fascinating information, she realized her detective work was far from finished. There was a great deal more to be known about Dr. Bradley Eliot, neurosurgeon-turned-newspaper mystery man than the last few minutes had revealed. But now that she had something to start with, uncovering the rest shouldn't be too much trouble. All she had to do was a little research. Call the Chicago paper, perhaps. Or . . .

Chicago! Of course! Why call when she had the best excuse in the world for going there? Her mouth curved upward in a catlike smile.

Bless you, big sister, she thought, for having your concert at such a convenient time in such a convenient place.

The sound of the water being turned off in the bathroom put an end to her quicksilver planning. Hastily but with great care she folded up the newswire copy and replaced it in the billfold. She was sitting non-chalantly in the easy chair, her legs crossed provocatively, when Brad, his hair damp and ruffled, his muscular body naked save for the towel he'd draped around his waist, entered the room. He stopped in surprise when he realized he was not alone.

"Hello," Lorie said tranquilly. Her eyes went to the towel and back up to his face. "Looks well on you."

"It got so late. I didn't think you were coming." He met her eyes evenly.

"Glad you left the door unlocked."

"I wouldn't want you standing around out in the hall."

Lorie tapped the manila envelope on her lap with a long, red fingernail. "Going to read my book tonight?" Her voice was sure, mocking.

Brad shrugged. "Planned to."

"I want your honest opinion."

"You'll get it."

Lorie was thoughtful for a moment, uncertain as to how she should put what she wanted to say next. "I don't want the family to know about it," she said at last, her face the picture of daughterly concern.

"O.K. But why?"

She managed a charmingly guilty smile. "Little too much for them to handle right now."

"Afraid of shocking them?" Brad seemed amused.

Lorie ran her tongue across her red lips. "Might shock you, too," she warned suggestively.

He smiled. "I think I can handle it."

Lorie's eyes surveyed his strong, well-developed body. There wasn't an ounce of fat on him. He was obviously a man who took pride in his appearance and in his masculinity. "I think you can, too," she agreed appreciatively. "You're a very sexy man."

Brad walked over and took the envelope from her. "Be interesting to see what the book says about you," he mused as he inspected the thickness of the manuscript. He added with typical insensitivity, "I'll start reading as soon as you leave."

Lorie lifted herself from the chair and stood before him calmly. "That's not very subtle," she said, pouting prettily.

"Didn't mean it to be."

She nodded with good-natured resignation. "Well," she acquiesced, "I'll go along." She winked saucily. "Leave you to your discoveries."

As she passed him, she stood on tiptoe and kissed him lightly on the mouth. Then, as she moved purposefully toward the door, her hand flashed back and tugged at the towel wound around his waist. It came off in one swift movement, and Lorie, looking down at it, laughed delightedly.

Brad stood where he was, unamused but not embarrassed or angry. "I'll get even with you for that someday," he told her dryly, his dark eyes holding, to her mind, more of a promise than a threat.

She stopped laughing then. Her eyes never left his face as she walked slowly back to him, the towel dragging on the floor behind her. "What's wrong with now?" she whispered, her voice wavering as her breath came faster. She was dizzyingly aware of his body, clean and fresh-smelling from the shower. She was so close to him she could feel the warmth exuding from his smooth, tanned skin.

He can't turn me away, not now, she thought as her heart pounded uncontrollably and the palms of her hands grew damp with perspiration.

In the next instant she felt herself being pulled roughly toward him, his nakedness encircling her, enfolding her, his lips locking hungrily onto hers. This time, there was no pulling away. Lorie was lost in a wave of unbridled passion as he kissed her again and again, as his hands explored her body and pulled violently at her hair. She was as eager as he when he wordlessly flipped off the light and guided her firmly to the bed.

7

The huge concert hall was filled with activity and noise as patrons eagerly made their way to their seats and talked enthusiastically about the new artist they were about to see and the pleasurable evening that stretched before them.

On the drafty old stage Leslie nervously peeked through a slit in the heavy brocade curtain. Is it really true? she asked herself wonderingly. Am I really going to play for all these important-looking people tonight? People who have actually *paid* to hear me perform.

Her eyes scanned the auditorium until they lighted upon the reassuring sight of her parents and sisters, seated in the fifth row, looking proud and excited. I can't let them down, she prayed. After all these years of encouraging me, helping me—I've got to make it all worthwhile!

She looked at her father, so distinguished and handsome in his tuxedo and ruffled shirt. Oh, Dad, this is what you've been waiting for. This is the night your eldest daughter may "rise above the crowd," the way you've always said one of us would one day.

And, Mom . . . She turned a loving glance on her mother. If you only knew what all your compassion and understanding has meant to me all these years. You never pushed me to go out on dates the way some mothers push their daughters, never made me feel like an oddball because the only thing I wanted to do was

play the piano and listen to good music. If you had . . .
well, I might not be here tonight.

She smiled at the vision of Peg, very grown-up-
looking in a long gown, and positively starry-eyed as
her head turned as if on a swivel, breathlessly taking in
all the sights and sounds of the concert hall.

And next to Peg was Lorie, seated on the aisle,
wearing a low-cut black-velvet dress, appearing very
composed as she studied her program. Leslie had been
stunned when her second sister had suddenly announced she would be coming to Chicago after all.
She'd come home after doing her interviews last night,
too late for Les' pre-debut party, and said with heart-
warming enthusiasm that she'd succeeded in finding a
way to attend the concert and have her column appear
as well. "I've been working hard on it all day," she'd
said with a weary smile, "trying to get far enough ahead
to take a couple of days off."

"That's why you rushed off tonight?" Leslie had
been deeply touched by this gesture of sisterly affection.

Lorie had planted a quick, impulsive kiss on her
cheek. "Just can't bear to be cheated of my sister's
big-time debut."

Like the complete journalist she was, however,
she'd made a business trip out of it as well and had left
Genoa City early this morning—way before any of the
others—in order to have a whole day in Chicago to
do some research she said was important.

Lorie, you and I have had our differences, Leslie
thought, staring out at the young woman who was so
breathtakingly beautiful that several people stopped and
looked back as they passed her on their way down the
aisle, but it pleases me so much that we've become so
close since you returned from Europe. I've found I can
talk to you more openly than with any other member of
the family. You alone understand what I'm going
through right now, and you've given me such wonderful advice about Brad.

Brad. Once again his name, exploding in her mind

like a Roman candle on the Fourth of July, knocked all other thoughts and concerns out of her head. Though he hadn't been able to be in the audience, Les felt he was with her in spirit at this moment, so linked was he with what was about to happen just two or three minutes from now. She'd talked to him this morning, just before leaving Genoa City, and as usual, he'd given her the gentle reassurance she needed to cast off her fears and doubts and push her onto that stage to give the best performance of her life.

"I promise you, Leslie," he'd said earnestly (almost, she allowed herself to imagine, lovingly), "the moment you touch that keyboard you'll become oblivious to a stage, musicians, an audience. And you'll be consumed with only one thing: sharing the richness of your God-given talent with the world. And that," he'd added quietly, "is much more than an honor. It's a responsibility. Especially today. Heaven knows it's what we all need now quite desperately. Someone, something, to believe in. Someone honest and decent and trustworthy, who deserves our support. With a kind of spiritual quality. And a different, more wholesome set of values." He'd looked at her then and smiled. "To me, Leslie, you epitomize all of those things."

How she had loved him at that moment! How she had longed to throw herself into his arms and cover that wonderful, beautiful face with kisses of gratitude and love! I know Lorie's right, she told herself guiltily, dropping the curtain and gazing wistfully into the darkness of the wings. I know I should keep my feelings to myself, do everything I can to keep from frightening him away by the intensity of my emotions. But I don't know how much longer I can hold back. Someday, somehow, Brad Eliot is going to know how very much I love him.

"Leslie? Are you ready?" Maestro Fautsch's thickly accented voice brought her back down to earth, back to the musty old stage where, she realized with a start, the orchestra was gathered, tuning their various instruments. She smoothed her shimmering white gown and flexed her fingers.

Can I do it? she asked herself as a blur of panic swept over her. Can I, Leslie Brooks, actually go out on that stage and perform for two solid hours? She sucked in her breath. The maestro was looking at her anxiously. "Yes," she told him shakily, "I'm ready."

"Good. We begin." He smiled broadly. "Tonight, my dear, there will be a new star in the heavens."

He turned and walked onto the stage. Leslie was in shadow as the great curtains swept open and the applause that rang through the hall pounded in her ears.

"Good evening, ladies and gentlemen," she heard Maestro Fautsch say, his usually soft voice sounding oddly unfamiliar as it boomed out over the mike. "Tonight, the Mid-America Symphony has a very special treat to offer you. You are going to be witnessing the debut of one of the most extraordinary young talents of our time. Listen. And be aware of the wonderful thing you will be hearing." He stretched a welcoming arm toward Leslie. "Miss Leslie Brooks."

God, be with me. So many wonderful people believe in me. Please don't let me fail them. Don't let me freeze up. Don't let me panic.

Her prayers were all she had to sustain her as she walked to the piano, another swell of applause washing over her like a great, encompassing wave. She sat on the bench and rearranged her dress around her. She felt for the pedals with her feet. She adjusted her position.

Suddenly the keyboard rose up grotesquely before her, like something out of a psychedelic dream. It was so huge! So forbidding! She looked at it in horror. How could she ever expect to handle a thing like that?

She heard the maestro tap his music stand with his baton. Her head snapped up attentively. All eyes were upon him as he raised the baton and held it in midair before bringing it down with a flourish that brought forth the crash of familiar music.

Leslie sat very still as the orchestra played the first bars of Rachmaninoff's *First Piano Concerto*. Her ears listened carefully for the cue that would herald her beginning. Her stomach twisted, her mouth felt unbearably dry. And then, without warning, a beautiful voice crept ever so softly over her mind.

"I promise you, Leslie, the moment you touch that keyboard you'll become oblivious to a stage, musicians, an audience. And you'll be consumed with only one thing: sharing the richness of your God-given talent with the world."

Like a weary, lost traveler who has just seen a light in a farmhouse window, she smiled a beatific smile. And attacked the keyboard with love and joyful self-assurance.

Lorie kept her eyes on the stage, but her gaze was glassy and she had to stifle a bored yawn. She supposed Leslie was doing a good job up there; God knew she looked intense enough, bent tautly over the keyboard, her hands flying, her mouth set in an expression of deep concentration. And she looked pretty decent, too—Lorie would give her that—in her silvery-white gown, her hair piled high on her head and hanging in little tendrils around her face and at the nape of her neck.

But Lorie really wasn't very interested in her sister at this moment. In fact, she'd have given anything if she'd been able to get out of attending this damned concert. She'd much rather be back in her hotel room mulling over all she'd learned today and working on putting together the pieces of the puzzle named Brad Elliot.

This little trip to Chicago has been most productive, she thought to herself with a satisfied smile. She'd started out the day by paying a visit to the file room of the Chicago *News*. She'd asked for a copy of the paper dated the same date she'd seen on Brad's newswire copy, and the clerk, a little balding man with a bulbous purple nose, had obligingly produced it for her. Unfortunately, the paper had contained little more infor-

mation than the newswire, so, upon returning to her
hotel suite, she was forced to put Plan Two into action.

Plan Two was a visit to Barbara Anderson, the
nurse and part-time model who had identified the
dead man's body as Brad Eliot. Lorie knew she'd have
had to have known Brad pretty well to have been asked
to make an identification like that, so she'd picked up
the telephone and called Northwestern Memorial Hospital, where the *News* article said she worked.

She hadn't given her real name, of course. She'd
told Barbara her name was Pat Bowes and that she was
a patient of Dr. Eliot who had been away for a while
and had only just learned of his tragic death. Although
Barbara hadn't shown much interest in talking with her,
Lorie had said it would mean a great deal to her if she
could just learn a little more about the accident and
about how Brad had spent his last weeks of life, and
Barbara had finally agreed to see her on her lunch
break.

Lorie had been taken aback when she'd walked into the hospital cafeteria and seen the statuesque blonde
who had hurried over to meet her. But then she realized
she should have expected it; anyone Brad Eliot became
involved with would have to be pretty damned special.
She'd adopted a very careful attitude with Barbara, trying hard to give the impression that her interest in Brad
stemmed from the great respect she'd had for him during the time she'd been under his care.

"He did more for me than I could possibly tell
you," she'd said, looking genuinely grieved and twisting
a handkerchief in carefully feigned agitation as she
spoke.

"He was a great doctor," Barbara had replied
quietly.

"I came back—hoping to see him again. Now . . ."

Barbara's blue eyes had grown wistful and Lorie
knew without a doubt that this girl could give her all
the answers she wanted. If only she *would!* "So many
hopes died with him," she'd said sadly.

"It must have been a terrible shock to his family." Go carefully, Lorie had admonished herself. Don't let her see you're after something.

"It was horrible for everyone who knew him."

"The paper mentioned his parents."

Barbara had nodded, a little ironically, Lorie thought. "That's all the family he had," she'd said softly.

"I never knew. Was Dr. Eliot ever married?" Lorie kept her eyes wide and innocent. This was dangerous ground; it would be easy to make a slip here.

Barbara suspected nothing. "Never," she'd said simply.

"What was he doing out in Ohio?" This was another thing Lorie wanted to get to the bottom of. The paper had said he'd made no mention of plans to leave town, had had several operations scheduled for the next day.

"I don't know," Barbara told her. Her blue eyes grew troubled, almost frightened. And suddenly she had begged to end the interview. "This is all very difficult for me, Miss Bowes," she'd said in a choked voice.

Lorie had leaned back and eyed her carefully. The girl was showing a great deal of emotion. Her relationship with Brad must have been very involved indeed. "The paper called you close friends," she offered, trying to appear deeply sympathetic. "But I can tell it was more than that."

Tears welled up in Barbara's eyes, and she looked down at the table in an attempt to keep them from showing. "So much more," she whispered.

Lorie nodded understandingly. "You loved him." She reached out and touched the nurse's hand.

The statement unleashed the dam of control, and Barbara's tears spilled over, unbated. "He's been dead a year," she said, sobbing, rubbing her wet cheeks with her hands, "and I'm still in love with him."

What would you say if you knew he was alive and living just a short plane ride from here? Lorie had wondered irreverently, still being very careful to maintain her sympathetic pose. What would you say if you knew that only last night he had taken me in his arms and made mad, passionate, wildly exciting love to me in a dreary little room over a restaurant? She put on an expression of deep sadness. "With a man like Brad, it isn't easy to forget," she said, and here, at least, she was being honest.

"There was too much left undone," Barbara had replied, struggling to get hold of herself again. "Too much left unsaid. Now he's dead and all I can do is mourn for him."

Going over the conversation in her mind, Lorie's thoughts returned again and again to the moment in which she'd asked the nurse why Brad had left Chicago on the day of his death. Barbara had said she didn't know. But the way in which she had changed the subject . . .

There's still a big mystery to be solved here, Lorie mused as her sister's fervent playing resounded in her ears. Brad Eliot was running away from something the day that car skidded and burned outside of Akron. Former girl friends may try to keep it a secret, but the woman who's going to win him is going to find out what it is!

8

Brad spread the reviews out across his desk and studied them, as he had done repeatedly since they had come across the teletype early this morning.

"Audience rewards Leslie Brooks with standing ovation. . . . Miss Brooks' impeccable, even glittering, technique was firmly based on emotional depth and comprehension remarkable in one so young. . . . One of the most auspicious debuts in this reviewer's long memory. . . ."

He smiled warmly. It had all been as he'd said it would be. The insecure, frightened little duckling had turned into a beautiful swan. You're on your way, Les, he congratulated her mentally. You need never be afraid again.

Naturally, the Brooks family was thrilled to death about her success. Stuart had invited him to the house for a welcome-home party this evening, and even Lorie had arrived at the office this morning babbling about how fantastic the evening had been and how beautifully her sister had handled the avalanche of praise that had been heaped on her head at the celebration afterwards.

Lorie. His brow wrinkled as she sprang, like a bright, beautiful bird, into his thoughts. If ever there was a woman who could exasperate and enchant a man at the same time, it was volatile, capricious, high-handed, delicious Lauralee Brooks. He had known her for over a month now—had been working side by side with her at the paper every day—and he still wasn't sure just what he thought of her. At times she could be the most audacious, impudent, annoying little bitch he'd ever met in his life. And then, suddenly, she'd turn soft and womanly, and her green eyes would look at him invitingly, and her mouth would turn up in that teasing, provocative smile, and he'd want to take her into his arms and squeeze her until the breath was knocked out of her and kiss the living hell out of those sensuous, mocking lips.

And he had done exactly that, he reflected soberly, more than once. The intimate moments they'd shared in his room couldn't exactly be called love-making—they were too wild and reckless, too devoid of real tenderness and gentleness for that. But since two nights ago, when she'd ripped the towel from around his waist and they'd come to know each other in a crazy, exciting way, he had admit his feelings for her were becoming more and more affectionate.

He had to admit, too, that she was a hell of a lot more talented and serious about her work than he'd first thought. That book she'd written in Europe was good. Not his cup of tea, really, as those things went. It was one of those commercial sex epochs where people jump in bed at the drop of a shoulder strap and do everything imaginable to one another with eager enthusiasm and abandon. But for what it was, it was damned good, and if she ever got it published, which she was bound and determined to do, it would probably be a best seller.

He'd been working with her on the polishing of it. Some of her characters he'd found inconsistent and there was a good bit of overwriting. But he was going to do what he could to help her set it straight.

Yes, Lauralee was a remarkable woman. Not, of course, in the way that Leslie was remarkable. Lorie didn't have that awesome spiritual quality that Les had that made her the beautiful artist she was, but she had a regular genius for sizing up the qualities she *did* have and making them work for her in a definite, somewhat dazzling way.

Think of the she-devil, he thought wryly, as Lorie —as if on cue—swung into the bullpen and made straight for his desk, throwing her arms around his neck and bestowing a light kiss on his forehead before he had time to be concerned as to whether anyone was watching. She had taken an early-morning flight out of Chicago.

"Reading about big sister, I see," she said dryly as her eyes went to the reviews still spread out before him.

"And feeling kind of proud," he replied, smiling.

"That's right." Lorie unwound her arms from his neck and pursed her lips thoughtfully. "You really made it possible."

Brad shook his head and began to fold up the newswire copy. "It was her talent."

"She couldn't have done it without you," Lorie persisted, her voice holding, to his mind, the tiniest hint of bitterness.

"I helped a little with her anxieties, that's all." He turned to her expectantly, wondering whether she'd come to discuss something with him, but her face was still thoughtful, her eyes studying him.

"Brad?" she said after a long moment of deliberation. "Are you in love with my sister?"

He was thrown by her directness, and he had to hold himself in tight to keep his discomfort from showing. "Did I say that?" he replied, carefully avoiding committing himself one way or the other.

Lorie continued to stare at him, her brow wrinkling speculatively. "All right, then," she amended, "do you want her to *think* you're in love with her? Or, more to the point, do you want *her* to fall in love with *you?*"

Brad met her eyes. "Your point?" he asked evenly.

Lorie was very earnest, very serious. "Leslie's where she wants to be now," she told him. "Everything's going great for her."

"Her *career* is going great," Brad corrected. There was a lot more in a woman's life than simply work.

"That's all that matters to her," Lorie insisted with a shrug.

Brad frowned. "You're sure of that?" As dedicated to her music as Leslie was, she had never seemed to him like a hardcore career woman.

"All I can do is tell you what she told me. She's determined to devote her life to her music. She thinks a man would simply complicate and upset her life."

"She told you that?" Brad was oddly disturbed.

Lorie nodded. "She doesn't believe a musician can divide her interests between a career and a husband. And, to Les, love means a husband."

Brad was thoughtful. The words had a good deal of truth to them. "I agree," he said slowly. "Love would mean total commitment to your sister."

Lorie's face became troubled. "But she's only human, Brad," she said with a sort of urgent appeal in her voice. "If you continue to pay so much attention to her, she might fall in love with you, and that would really confuse her. She's used you as a crutch. Your relationship with her served a good purpose. But she can stand on her own two feet now."

She stopped and waited for a response, but Brad said nothing, simply sat looking at her concernedly. "Unless, of course," she added crisply, "you're in love with her. Then you should go after her." She offered a cold, brittle smile. "You'd know soon enough if it's music or you that's the most important."

Brad sighed. He guessed she was right.

"Look, could we change the subject for now?" Lorie asked suddenly, her voice lightening, her face becoming more relaxed. "I came over here to ask a favor of you."

"What's that?" Brad, still disturbed, was relieved not to have to respond to her cool challenge.

"These family get-togethers like the one we're having tonight get to be a little much. I wondered . . ." Her eyes fixed themselves on him appealingly. "When you leave the house, would you take me along? I'm happy for Les, I'm very proud of her, but enough is enough. I don't care where we go or what we do," she added guilelessly. "But, please, would you bail me out? I know Les will understand."

He had to smile in spite of himself. Poor Lorie. She was trying so hard to show some family loyalty, but Les' success was still niggling at her. Well, he guessed he could understand that. He'd never had brothers or sisters, but he imagined sibling rivalry could be pretty rough going at times

"Of course," he told her genially. "When I go, I'll whisk you along beside me." He was genuinely touched by the look of gratitude in her eyes.

Leslie sat amid multicolored balloons and hanging crepe-paper streamers feeling both foolish and proud. The family had gone all out to give her a bang-up homecoming, and she was pleased—for their sake— that Maestro Fautsch had allowed her to come home for a couple of days instead of going right on to Detroit to prepare for the next concert.

For herself, she really didn't like having such a fuss made about her. She was glad the family was excited about her success in Chicago, but she was just the same old Leslie after all, and she wished everyone would just go on treating her that way.

Of course, there was one redeeming factor about this party. Brad Eliot was there. Stuart, knowing his interest in her music, had invited him to join the family, and here he was, sitting comfortably in the Brooks living room like an honored guest. Les knew her mother wasn't exactly thrilled when she learned he'd be coming, but tonight was so special that Les thought she'd be willing to accept almost anything as long as everyone was happy.

"Must have been a fantastic evening," Brad was saying to her, his warm brown eyes reflecting the happiness she knew he felt for her.

"I . . . I can't even begin to describe what I felt,"

she told him a little breathlessly. "The utter euphoria. Then, when it was over, standing up there—the applause and everything. I was sobbing like a baby." She sighed, and a wistful smile crossed her face. "It was a night I'll never forget."

"And, Brad," Lorie interjected, sounding genuinely impressed, "you should have seen the way she was *mobbed* at the party afterwards. She was surrounded by handsome musicians!"

Leslie blushed. She was grateful for her sister's enthusiasm, but she wished the family wouldn't keep breaking in that way. What she really wanted was to be alone with Brad. It had been so long since they'd had one of their walks. Maybe if she could find a way to get him alone, she could suggest going out for a bit of air.

"They were just being kind," she said modestly, in response to Lorie's observation. "It was nothing."

Suddenly, Jennifer rose and began to clear away the cups and dessert plates. "I hope you don't mind, Mr. Eliot," she said politely. "I just want to get these things in the dishwasher."

"Not at all," Brad replied. "It was very sweet of you to have me here." He got up from his chair and extended a respectful hand to Stuart. "Stuart, thanks for giving me the chance to congratulate Leslie."

Stuart smiled. "It was good having you here, Brad."

Leslie's heart plummeted. He was leaving! Without giving her the chance to suggest that walk.

"We are, all of us, very proud of you, Les," he said to her, bending over and bestowing a soft kiss on her brow. Her disappointment was so overwhelming that she couldn't even take pleasure in the feel of his lips on her skin. "Must you go so soon?" she asked plaintively.

Before he could answer, Lorie jumped up from the chair next to his and said to him familiarly, "I'll get out coats."

Their coats? Hers and Brad's? Leslie's stomach

turned over as she heard the words. What was Lorie up to this time?

"I promised Lorie I'd help her with a project she's working on," Brad said, as if he'd just read her mind. He turned toward Lorie as she handed him her coat, and helped her shrug into it. "Good night, Mrs. Brooks," he said warmly. "Good night, Stuart. See you in the morning." He winked at Peg, who'd been eyeing him worshipfully all evening.

"Right, Brad," Stuart replied. He and Jen followed the two to the door while Leslie remained, as if transfixed, on the sofa.

Am I going crazy? she asked herself dazedly. Is this really happening—again? The first time Lorie had whisked Brad out from under her nose it had had to do with that silly business about the bet. And she'd been so contrite and apologetic when Les had lit into her about it that Les had ended up feeling guilty for being the tiniest bit suspicious. But what excuse could she possibly have for *this* little maneuver? She knew it was a special night for Leslie. She knew how Leslie felt about Brad. Didn't she know better than to go off with him like he was her own personal property?

She didn't know how long she remained there thinking about it, but by the time her mother's voice urged her to go on up to bed, she realized the living room had been tidied up and Jennifer was already in her robe.

"I thought I'd stay up and wait for Lorie," she said, wondering how she could have been so deep in thought that she hadn't even heard Peg removing the balloons and crepe paper. "We really haven't had a chance to talk yet."

"You may have a long wait," her mother said, a touch of disapproval in her voice. "She seems to be very fond of Mr. Eliot."

Les' head shot up. It was all she could do to keep her voice light and casual when she asked, "Do you think they've become good friends?"

Jennifer shook her head in disgust. "If they have, it's not a friendship I'd approve of," she grumbled.

"Has . . . has she seen a lot of Mr. Eliot?" Les could hear her own heart pounding in her ears as she waited fearfully for the answer.

"As far as I know, just at the office," her mother replied. "But," she added dryly, "I'm afraid Lorie doesn't take me into her confidence." Then she looked at Leslie and smiled. "Maybe she'll confide in you. I know she doesn't like me questioning her."

Leslie nodded, her face a carefully formed mask. "Tonight," she agreed in a cold, dead voice, "I think she'll talk to me."

She thought she'd go mad waiting for Lorie to come home. Each time the clock chimed the quarter hour she strained her ears for the sound of a car. Several times she walked over to the front window and stared out into the darkness. But Lorie seemed determined to keep her in suspense. It was almost one o'clock before her car turned into the driveway and her key turned in the front-door lock.

Leslie stood in the shadows of the hallway as her sister walked briskly inside, deftly unbuttoning her coat and tossing her brown-leather shoulder bag on the hall table. She stepped back in surprise as Les moved out into the light and confronted her with an accusing glare.

"Hi, Les," Lorie said cautiously, trying hard to act as if there were nothing unusual about her older sister waiting up for her at this late hour—though, of course, there was.

"What are you trying to pull, Lorie?" Leslie's voice cut sharply through the stillness of the sleeping house.

"What . . . what are you talking about?"

"I trusted you." Leslie hissed. "I confided in you. Told you I was in love with Brad."

"And I haven't told a soul," Lorie replied defensively. She calmly removed her coat and hung it in the closet.

"But you've been trying to charm him," Leslie

pointed out. *"Why,* Lorie? I know you don't care about him." She stopped and swallowed hard, her throat so tight she was afraid she wouldn't be able to go on. "Are you just trying to hurt me? Because you know I love him?"

Lorie looked at her. "You're being ridiculous, Les," she said in a flat, scornful voice. "Making a lot out of nothing. I don't care anything about him as a man."

"You take him away my first night at home," Les shot back. She had no intention of letting her sister dismiss *this* one so lightly. "When you have to know how much I wanted to be with him."

Lorie tossed her long chestnut hair. "We were working on something," she declared with a good deal of impatience. There was no regret in her manner this time. No wide eyes and protestations of innocence. "Believe it or not, Brad *is* helping me."

Leslie stared at her bitterly. How dumb did she think she was, anyway? "You told me how easy it was for you to do your column," she reminded her; like Lorie not giving an inch. "You don't need help with that."

Lorie regarded the blazing eyes for a long moment, and then she said intensely, as if bestowing a great gift, "Les, I'm going to confide in you. I'm writing a book. It means a lot to me."

Leslie was thrown. "Why is that so secret?" she demanded, sure there was a trick here somewhere.

"Because I don't want anyone to know until it's published. And, believe me, it's going to be published someday!"

Leslie felt the room spinning around her. A book! A secret book that Brad was helping her with! Was it true? Was she really wrong about Lorie this time too? If only she could be *sure.* . . .

"And that's all it is?" she asked helplessly. She felt almost disappointed.

"Brad helped *you,*" Lorie reminded her. "You're a big success now. You're where you want to be, thanks to him."

Leslie bit her lip. "I'm not denying that."

"So why should you resent it because he's helping me now? Are you so selfish you can't stand the idea of success for me, too?"

"I never said that!" Les retorted, stung. "You know I've always wanted you to get what you want out of life."

"Then don't accuse me of trying to steal your man just because he's helping me get what I want. My book means as much to me as your music means to you. Can't you understand that, for God's sake?"

"I can understand about the book," Leslie said, deflated. "But why did you have to go off with Brad tonight, of all nights?"

"I take his help when he has the time to give it." Lorie was making it all sound so simple, so right. "And he was willing to give it tonight."

Leslie turned and began to pace the floor, trying to sort out the confusion in her head. "I don't know what to think," she said, almost in tears.

Her sister's reply was annoyed and impatient. "You're a big star now, Leslie. You're not supposed to be an introverted little girl anymore. If you love the man, go to him. Tell him. But don't go around making all sorts of accusations and innuendos. I'm sick of it."

Looking very injured and indignant, Lorie squared her shoulders and proceeded to flounce up the staircase. She'd almost reached the top when Leslie, confused and miserable, called after her.

"Lorie . . ." She sounded like a little girl who'd just been punished for robbing the cookie jar.

"Yes?" Lorie turned around and looked down at her. "Now what?"

"If you *are* telling the truth . . ." Leslie's face was aflame. She felt awful. "Then . . . I'm sorry."

It didn't make her feel any better when, without a word of response, Lorie turned her back and continued stiffly up the stairs.

9

She didn't sleep for two nights straight, simply lay in her familiar old brass bed and thought about it over and over. Her suspicions and doubts consumed her. Brad's relationship with Lorie had taken on more importance than her concert in Detroit, Maestro Fautsch, anything.

She *had* believed Lorie when she'd said Brad was helping her with her book. She'd been miserable when Lorie had accused her of not being able to stand the idea of someone else having success. *Of course* she wanted Lorie to succeed. She hoped her book would be the greatest seller ever. But she knew what had developed from her own work with Brad. Lorie had said she didn't care for him as a man. But that could change. As she got to know him better, her whole attitude could be turned around.

And, as for Brad, he'd once told her he thought Lorie spoiled and selfish. But she was so gloriously beautiful most men could forgive her anything. Even people who started out not liking her often ended up eating out of her hand. And if she set her sights on Brad, set her mind toward pleasing him . . .

I have to do something, she decided as the dawn broke through her window on the morning of the day she was to leave for Detroit. I have to do something that will stop all these awful suspicions. I have to let Brad know how I feel about him so he can make his own choice. And if, in the end, it should turn out to be

Lorie . . . well, at least he would know there *had* been a choice.

The thing to do, she supposed, would be to call him and ask him to meet her this morning, maybe even drive her out to the airport. Then they could have a frank talk and she could tell him everything she'd been thinking and feeling for so long.

But could she do it? She turned onto her stomach and cradled her pillow in her arms. Could she actually look this gorgeous, wonderful man in the eye and say calmly, "Brad Eliot, I'm in love with you." The thought made her break out in little beads of perspiration. What would he say if she did? Suppose he looked at her in shock, in disgust even, and turned away, repulsed by her confession. Or suppose he laughed and asked how she could be stupid enough to fall in love with him when she knew he could never feel the same way about an ugly, insignificant little thing like herself?

Of course she knew Brad would never do any of those things. He was much too sensitive to people's feelings to ever repulse or mock her. But if she told him face to face, she would be able to see from the expression in his eyes what he was thinking. And if it was dismay . . . well, she simply couldn't bear it.

Why not write to him? The idea came to her in a flash, and she sat bolt upright as it grabbed on her consciousness. Yes! That was the answer! She wouldn't have to be there when he opened a letter; he could read what was in her heart and then they would go on from there. She would even enclose the complimentary ticket to the Detroit concert she'd asked Maestro Fautsch to get for her. And if he showed up . . . well, then she would know. Stealthily, so as not to wake the sleeping Lorie, she crept out of bed and pulled open the desk drawer where her stationery box was kept. Grabbing her robe, she took the box and tiptoed downstairs to the shadowy living room. She settled herself at the end of the sofa and, in the light of the end-table lamp, proceeded to write the most important letter of her life.

She began by telling him she had wanted to talk to him in person, but that the maestro hadn't allowed her much time at home before calling her to Detroit to rehearse for the next concert. And she mentioned the enclosed ticket, telling him she'd obtained it for him because he had told her how much he wanted to hear her play. And then—and here her pen wavered a bit—she poured out all her longing, all that she'd been afraid to tell him heretofore but simply couldn't hold back another moment. "I love you," she wrote, her heart constricting with each carefully formed letter. "If I see you in Detroit, I'll know whether I did the right thing in telling you."

By the time she had signed her name she was so full of trepidation that she didn't dare read it over; she simply folded it up around the ticket and stuffed it into the envelope. There, she told herself firmly as she moistened the glue with her tongue, the deed is done. Her eyes grew misty. And, oh, Brad . . . please, please be there!

She had fixed herself some coffee and was sitting in the kitchen sipping it thoughtfully when Lorie, usually the family's earliest riser, came down to make her breakfast.

"Hey, what're *you* doing up?" she asked lightly, the heels of her satin scuffs clicking on the linoleum as she swept across the floor in a billowing peignoir. "I thought all you celebrities slept till noon."

Les offered a weak smile. "Guess I'm a little jittery about Detroit."

Lorie gave her a scornful look. "Jittery? After the way things went in Chicago? Les, you have to be the most insecure person on earth."

"Lorie . . ." Les ignored the barb. She didn't want any misunderstandings at this point.

"Yes?" Lorie wasn't even looking at her. She was busily pouring ingredients for a health drink into the blender.

"Before I go, I want things to be right between us."

Lorie tossed her tangled hair. "You're the reason they're not," she said coldly.

Les looked down at her coffee. Her eyes were on the steaming blackness as she spoke. "I'm sorry I doubted you. It was foolish of me to make such a big thing out of your seeing Brad."

Lorie turned and faced her then. "You believe me now?" she asked, frowning.

"I don't blame you for wanting him to help you with your book." Leslie looked up at her, her guilt making her genuinely miserable.

Lorie began to thaw. "The man does have a good mind," she reminded her, reproachfully but no longer angry. "And I need all the help I can get. Just as you did, Les."

Leslie felt the sting and was filled with remorse. "I wish I hadn't jumped to conclusions," she mumbled.

"I wish you hadn't, too. I don't like us to be angry at each other." Lorie had finished mixing her drink now and was pouring it into a tall glass.

"I hate it, Lorie," Les said beseechingly. "Believe me, it spoiled my whole time home."

Lorie smiled and came over to give her a quick hug. "It's been rotten for me, too, big sister," she said affectionately.

"Then we can forget it?" Leslie looked at her appealingly.

"If you're sure you really understand my interest in Brad now."

"I understand it," Les assured her. Then, with an embarrassed little smile she added sheepishly, "Guess I love him so much I think other women have to feel the same way."

"You just keep on loving him, honey," Lorie told her with a conspiratorial wink. "As long as you let *me* pick his brains."

Les grinned. "It's a deal."

"And you'll trust me from now on?"

"I will." Leslie declared fervently. "I really will."

Lorie drained her frothy drink and put the glass in the sink. "We'll make up for this rotten time when you come home again," she told Leslie, adding distractedly, "Now I've got to dash upstairs and get dressed. Want to get some work done at the office before it gets too hectic." As she passed the kitchen table she noticed the envelope lying next to Les' coffee cup. "Want me to mail that for you?" she offered.

Leslie hesitated. It would be the easiest thing in the world for Lorie to take her letter to the newspaper and put it on Brad's desk. But . . . no. Even though she and her sister understood each other now, this matter was too close to her heart to have somebody know about it before Brad knew himself. "No, it's O.K.," she replied with a grateful smile. "I'll take care of it."

She had the envelope in her purse and was getting dressed herself when Peggy came dashing into her room to say good-bye.

"Knock 'em dead in Detroit!" she exclaimed, throwing her arms around Les in an enthusiastic embrace.

"I'll do my best," Leslie told her, trying not to laugh.

Peg grinned. "That'll be good enough."

As the youngster turned to go, Leslie had a sudden thought. She opened her purse and pulled out the letter, calling her sister back as she did so. "Do me a favor, Peg?" she asked. When Peg nodded her firey red head she held out the envelope. "Would you stop by the newspaper office and give this note to Brad Eliot?"

"Sure," Peggy replied. "Mark's picking me up. He can make the detour on our way to school." Mark, Leslie knew, was Peg's current best beau.

"You won't forget?" She knew Peg was trustworthy, but like any teenager she could be a little dizzy at times.

" 'Course not!" her sister declared importantly. She took the letter. "So long, big sister."

Leslie had no way of knowing that, once downstairs, Peg would hand the letter over to Lorie, sure, in her puppylike innocence, that if Les had known Lorie had forgotten something and come back to the house, she would have trusted her with this errand herself. After all, Lorie worked with Brad. What could be more natural than for *her* to deliver the letter?

Brad wasn't at his desk when Lorie arrived at the newspaper. Upon checking the assignment sheet tacked on the bulletin board, she saw that he was out gathering information for his series of articles on drugs in Genoa City and would be out most of the day. Satisfied that her deed would not be detected—at least by the person most directly affected—she sat down behind her own desk and carefully removed Leslie's letter from her purse. With one of her long fingernails she easily opened the envelope, making no attempt to keep the paper from ripping and showing signs of its having been tampered with. Her eyes glittering brightly, she pulled out the single sheet of paper, glancing briefly at the ticket that fell out with it, and put it on her desk. She smiled to herself as she read the words meant only for the eyes of Brad Eliot.

Dear Brad,
    I wanted so much to talk to you before I left. The evening you spent at our house was much too hectic for any real conversation. But Maestro Fautsch called me to Detroit sooner than I expected, so I have had to content myself with sending you this letter. You told me you wanted to hear me play, so I'm enclosing a ticket for the one evening performance we'll be giving in Detroit. You can't possibly know how happy it would make me if I come on stage and see you sitting in the front row, center-aisle seat. You can't know how I'll feel, Brad, because I've never had the courage to tell you before, but—I love you. There, I've said what's been in my heart for so long. If I see you in Detroit, I'll know whether I did the right thing in telling you.
                                                    Leslie

Lorie clicked her tongue against her teeth and gave a cynical little laugh. "I told you, dear sister," she said, speaking aloud to the stationery as if it were an extension of Leslie, "it's bad psychology to tell a man you love him." She folded it up and replaced it in her purse, along with the torn envelope and ticket. Oh Peg, she thought to herself, inwardly laughing in delight, how right you were to give it to *me* to deliver!

10

Brad was disappointed, and not a little hurt. Leslie's Detroit concert was tonight, and she hadn't even called him before she left Genoa City to say good-bye. He thought sure she'd want to get in touch with him; she'd always called before leaving town in the past. And just before she went to Chicago, they'd talked about his catching the Detroit concert. Why hadn't Les reminded him of that? Didn't she want him to hear her play after all?

If he didn't know her so well, he might think that her success in Chicago had gone to her head, that now that she was a star she didn't need any of her old friends anymore. But Les wasn't like that, could never be like that. The relationship Brad had established with her was deep and strong, and he was sure she wouldn't turn her back on it just because she'd at last found some confidence and had no need of his encouragement and praise.

He remembered what Lorie had told him the other day about Leslie's music being her whole life. Perhaps that was what was causing her to act so aloof these days. Perhaps she was just so absorbed in her music that her mind didn't even encompass anything else. But, there again, that sort of thing just wasn't like Leslie. She was very involved in her career, yes. But in the months they'd gotten to know each other, Brad had seen another side of her, too, a very strong womanly, even maternal side. Leslie Brooks, he felt sure, was

a girl who wanted more out of life than a string of
concerts and the continuous ring of applause in her
ears.

Still, Lorie had told him that Les had said she intended to devote her life to her music, that she didn't
believe a musician could divide her interests between a
career and a husband. And she'd even advised him to
ease out of her sister's life now that she was set on
the path to fame because she might confuse his friendship with love and feel threatened by it. Was *that* the
reason she hadn't called him? Was she blocking him
out of her life in order to make certain he wouldn't
pose a threat to her ambitions where her career was
concerned?

If so, he was sorry. He'd never led Leslie to believe there was anything romantic in his feelings toward
her. In fact, he'd bent over backwards to keep their
walks and late suppers as platonic as possible, rarely
even taking her hand, and kissing her on the cheek a
few times in strictly brotherly fashion.

Not that he'd particularly wanted it that way, he
reflected as he deftly maneuvered his car through the
wintry, snowy streets and the slow-moving evening traf-
fic. There had been times when Leslie's sweetness, her
classic beauty, her heartrending vulnerability had gone
straight to his heart and he'd wanted to take her in his
his arms, kiss her long and lingeringly, and tell her she
need never be afraid, that he'd always be around to
care for and protect her. But he hadn't done it—partly,
he realized, because, like Lorie, he had sensed she
couldn't handle a thing like that at this point. He
didn't know whether her feelings for him could ever
be kindled into real love, but he knew that if they
should be, she would commit herself to him totally.
And *he* couldn't handle that. There was no one who
would make a better wife than Leslie Brooks, that much
he knew for sure. But as long as he was still dealing
with the problems he'd left behind in Chicago, as long
as there were things he couldn't open up to anyone

about, he had to stay clear of romantic entanglements. Especially with a vulnerable girl like Les.

Now, Lorie, that was different, he thought with a rakish smile. He and Lorie were involved—at least in the sexual sense of the word—but it was a strictly-for-laughs thing. Lorie Brooks couldn't center her life around a man any more than she could play *Beethoven's Third* on the zither. Her life was—and always would be—centered around Lorie Brooks. She considered men pleasant diversions, toys that could be played with and discarded, that was all. And at this point, a toy was all he wanted to be. Someone to play with, have fun with, no strings attached.

Yes, this relationship with Lorie suited him fine. She was an intelligent girl, interesting to talk to, stimulating to be with. And the female side of her was dynamite. She was an exciting and enthusiastic lover, yet she was not in the least possessive—something he found most appealing at this point in his life. He had no qualms about continuing the affair with her for as long as it stayed just the way it was and nobody got hurt.

He was on his way now to her new apartment, which she'd rented yesterday with the impulsiveness that marked her mercurial personality. Of course, he hadn't been surprised that she'd wanted her own place. Lorie wasn't the kind of girl who would be happy living in the watchful bosom of a concerned family. She was too much of a free spirit; she needed a place of her own, where she could come and go as she pleased, see whom she pleased, do *what* she pleased. It was just that, he mused, frowning, she might have stayed at home a *little* longer, considering how long she'd been away from the family when she went to Paris.

Oh, well, far be it from me to judge Lorie, he told himself as he turned into the parking lot of her new, modern building. As she's informed me many times, she does her own thing. There's no way I'd try to tell her how to run her life.

The apartment, when he got there, was strewn

with cartons, suitcases, garment bags, hatboxes, and all the things an apartment is usually strewn with when one is moving in or out. Lorie herself, however, was unchaotically beautiful, greeting him warmly in a tight-fitting pants outfit, her soft hair, brushed to a silky sheen, falling sexily around her shoulders.

"I'll fix us drinks," she told him when she'd taken his coat and had cleared a place for him on the heavily littered sofa. "No," she retracted as her eye fell on the carton of soft drinks that was sitting on the floor next to the coffee table. "First, you'd better lift that."

She showed him where she wanted it—on a shelf she'd already set up as a bar—and then she rummaged through it until she found a bottle of club soda. "Two Scotch and sodas coming up," she said gaily, dropping in the ice cubes and mixing the drinks with studied expertise.

"Here's to Brad." She grinned as she handed him his glass. "May you live as long as you want to—and want to as long as you live!"

Brad smiled. She never failed to amuse him with her pseudo-sophisticated act. "I'll drink to that," he said wryly. After he'd drunk, he held out his glass to her. "Here's to . . ." He hesitated as he deliberated whether to say the words that came to mind. "Lorie," he finished abruptly.

As always, her lightening perception picked up on his uncertainty. "What were you *going* to say?" she demanded.

He sighed and capitulated. "It was going to be, 'Here's to Lorie's liberated life.' "

"I like it!" Her green eyes shone and her smile displayed her perfect white teeth. "Why'd you edit it?"

He answered her seriously. "Didn't think you should drink to it unless it's what you really want."

"It is," she assured him.

"Careful, Lorie," he cautioned. "There's an old Arab proverb . . ." He shook his head uncertainly. "Some say it's an old Chinese proverb. Anyway, it's old. It goes: 'Be sure of what you really want because it's what you're going to get.' "

"Lovely." Lorie smiled. "A liberated life is what I really want."

"As long as you're never sorry."

Lorie looked at him and grinned, "My motto is 'Better sorry than safe.' "

Brad chuckled then. There was no talking to this girl. "How about one more toast?" he suggested.

Lorie raised her glass. "What?" she asked, her eyes sparkling at him.

He cleared his throat. "To Leslie, and a successful concert in Detroit tonight."

Lorie laughed and took a small sip. "We're toasting a sure thing, of course," she observed.

Brad nodded. "As sure as talent and hard work can make it." He swigged his drink and added a little bitterly, "Would've liked to have been there to see it —except for the little matter of the ticket she promised and forgot to send me."

"Oh, there'll be lots and lots of tickets," Lorie said. "Now . . . you've toasted me and I've toasted you, and we've both toasted Leslie." She raised her glass again. "Here's to *us*."

They drank, and then she put him to work hanging a picture. He expected her to keep him busy the rest of the evening, but once the picture was hung, she surprised him by asking him to take her back to his room at Pierre's.

"I left my typewriter and manuscript there, remember?" she reminded him. "We're going to get them tonight—and I'm going to snow you with questions about the chapter we left off on."

He shook his head. The girl was damned serious about her book, nobody could deny that. "O.K.," he agreed affably. At least *someone* in the Brooks family wanted his help right now.

Leslie arrived at the theater early. She couldn't possibly wait around, doing nothing, in her hotel room when she was expecting the evening to bring the most important event in her life. Oh, Brad, she thought longingly as she walked onto the darkened stage and peered out through the peephole in the curtain at the still, empty auditorium. One hour now until I see you. I'll walk out on this stage and look into your eyes . . . front row, center aisle. You'll be there. You would've let me know if anything had stopped you from coming. And that makes tonight the most important night of my life. My love . . . my love. . . .

She stood riveted to the spot as the first sprinkling of patrons entered the theater and spoke in hushed tones as they made their way to their plush, red-velvet seats. Each time a lone male form appeared, her heart stopped, and then slowly began to beat again as she realized it was someone else—not the man she was waiting so eagerly to see.

The hands of the old backstage clock moved steadily forward, and almost before she knew it it was seven-thirty. He'll be here any minute now, she thought, her stomach tightening in delicious anticipation.

Seven-forty-five. And still no sign of him. Could his plane have been delayed? she wondered anxiously, beginning now to feel the first seeds of doubt. Could something have happened at the newspaper to detain him? But, no, she was sure he'd have called if anything were keeping him from making it to the concert. Brad was a gentleman in every sense of the word. He wouldn't just leave her dangling, no matter what.

Eight o'clock. The auditorium was full now, the one lone seat on the front row center aisle looking conspicuously empty. Where are you, Brad? she asked herself, almost frantic now. The curtain is about to go up. You must be here on time. You must!

"If you are ready, my child, it is time to begin." Maestro Fautsch was standing behind her, gently pulling her away from the curtain with a reassuring hand.

Her heart fell. "Could we wait a few more minutes, Maestro?" She turned to him and saw the doubt on his face. "Please, Maestro. Just a few more minutes."

He studied her carefully, his kindly old brow wrinkling in concern. Then he leaned past her and peered out through the curtain. "The man for whom you wanted the ticket—he is not yet here?"

Leslie shook her head. Her eyes begged him to agree to the delay. She had told the maestro there was someone special in her life. He knew how important it was for her to have him here tonight.

"Very well, dear child," he conceded with an indulgent smile. "A few more minutes."

Leslie squeezed his hand in gratitude and turned back to the curtain. He'll be here, she told herself with fervent conviction. I'm sure Peg gave him my letter. I know she followed through. She glanced back at the clock. Four minutes past eight. If he were coming, he should have been there. Maybe, she decided, she should phone his room in Genoa City. Just to satisfy herself that he was really on his way.

She dug some change out of her purse and hurried over to the pay phone in the wings. With trembling fingers she dialed the number she had long since memorized. He won't be there, she thought, feeling a little guilty checking up on him this way. No one will answer the phone.

To her surprise, the ringing was interrupted by the receiver being lifted at the other end.

"Hello?" The answering voice was not Brad's— but a woman's. Leslie caught her breath and gripped the phone more tightly in her hand. It sounded like . . . it *couldn't* be . . . !

"Lorie?" she asked in stunned disbelief.

"Yes?" Her sister's voice was cool and matter-of-fact. "Leslie?"

Leslie swallowed hard. There must be an explanation. Maybe Lorie was watering his plants or something.

"Is Brad on his way to Detroit?" she asked, knowing in her heart there wasn't a plant on earth that couldn't survive a night without watering.

"No," Lorie replied. "He's here."

"But . . ." Leslie's mind was all confusion. *There?* In *Genoa City?* "My letter . . ."

Lorie sounded very impatient. "Don't know what you're talking about, Les," she told her briskly.

"What . . . what are you doing in Brad's room?"

Her sister's reply was straightforward and to the point. "Brad's helping me with my book," she said. As if that explained everything. His ignoring the ticket. Failing to call. Everything.

"Let me speak to him." Les' head was beginning to ache.

"Can't," Lorie replied. "He's downstairs in the restaurant at the moment."

Leslie was silent. Her sister! With Brad on the night she expected him in Detroit! On the night she expected to reaffirm her love for him! "What are you trying to do to me, Lorie?" she cried, her voice an agonized wail.

"Just stop it, Leslie!" Lorie shouted. Les could tell by her tone that she felt she was being done an injustice again.

But she wasn't going to let her get away with her lies this time. "Tell me!" she demanded fiercely. "What are you trying to do to me?"

Lorie waited a long time before she answered. And then her voice came across the line loud and clear. "*I'm* not trying to do anything to you, Leslie," she declared. "Isn't it just possible that Brad is interested in *me?*"

Leslie felt her hand go limp and she had to clutch at the receiver to keep from dropping it. "What're you telling me?" she asked, so weak she could scarcely speak.

She could almost see Lorie's smug smile. "I think," her sister told her, "you get the message."

"I . . . I . . ." She was stammering, trying to think of a rejoinder, trying desperately not to believe what she was hearing.

"Leslie, dear . . ." Suddenly it was Maestro Fautsch's voice in her ear. She turned and faced him dully. "We cannot keep our audience waiting any longer." He held out an arm for her to take. "Come, my dear."

Torn as to what she should do, she looked at him and then looked at the phone in her hand. Should she say something more to Lorie? Rage at her? Accuse her of stealing Brad, of lying all this time? She took a shaky breath. No. Because the fault was not all Lorie's. Brad had read her letter. He knew she was waiting for him. He had made his choice. Slowly she hung up the phone, and like an automaton who does not see or feel but responds only to direction, she took the Maestro's arm.

She found herself on the stage, seated at the piano, the bright overhead lights glaring down on her. She heard the introductory bars of the orchestra. She heard her cue. Automatically, her fingers found the keys and flew expertly across the board. She didn't know whether she was playing the correct notes or not. She wasn't aware of anything but indescribable pain and her sister's voice pounding in her ears. "I'm not trying to do anything to you, Leslie. Isn't it just possible that Brad is interested in me?"

She shook her head violently, as if to throw out the words. But they kept coming back, louder and louder—and she felt as if she were drowning in them. Brad is interested in me. Brad interested in me. Brad interested in me. . . .

She was aware of her fingers faltering on the keys. She couldn't seem to keep them steady now. Brad and me, Lorie's voice screamed relentlessly. Brad and me.

She didn't know when it happened, but suddenly the music stopped. She looked down at her hands. They were hanging lifelessly at her sides. She studied them dazedly. What were they doing there? They should be on the keyboard.

She felt the touch of a gentle hand on her shoulder

and looked up. As if in a haze, Maestro Fautsch's face danced before her. He looked worried. Worried . . . and shocked.

"I'm sorry," she mumbled feebly. "I'm sorry." She felt the hand lifting her now, helping her up from the piano bench, and gently guiding her off the stage. She heard a smattering of applause coming from the direction of the audience, and then a buzz of excited whispers.

"I'm terribly, terribly sorry." She was in her hotel suite, though she had no recall of being taken there. Things were beginning to clear a little. The hazy feeling was gone. She felt mortified. What had she done tonight?

"What happened, Leslie?" Maestro Fautsch was asking worriedly.

"I . . . I don't know exactly. I was playing, and suddenly everything froze."

The maestro looked at her intently. "Do you know why?"

Brad, she thought, agonized. I was so sure you'd be there. I poured my heart out to you. Such a fool. . . . She shook her head. She'd never tell anyone what a fool she'd been. Never. "I feel so humiliated," she said wretchedly. "How could I do that to the orchestra? To you?"

"I am not concered about the orchestra or me." Dear Maestro Fautsch. As usual, this wonderful man was standing by her. "You've been under too much strain," he said soothingly. "I should never have called those extra rehearsals."

"No! No!" she assured him quickly. "It has nothing to do with you."

"What is it then?" Maestro Fautsch was almost as distressed as she.

She bit her lip. Brad. Didn't phone. Didn't write. Nothing. Empty seat. Such a fool. "Something personal," she answered.

"I thought so. Leslie," the maestro begged, "unburden yourself. Tell me what it is."

She looked at him. His dark eyes were full of concern. She hesitated. Such a fool! "It was a phone call," she confessed at last.

"Somebody called you?"

She shook her head.

"You called someone?"

"Yes." Leslie swallowed. Her throat felt like sandpaper. "Yes."

"And the person told you something?"

"Yes, yes."

"What was it?" Maestro Fautsch was looking at her expectantly.

"I . . . uh . . . uh . . ." Leslie started to speak, then broke off, her lips trembling. "Don't make me go on, please."

The maestro stared at her for a moment, and then he put a protective arm around her shoulders and led her gently toward the bedroom. "Very well, Leslie," he replied. "I will not press you further. But you must rest."

"Rest," Leslie repeated gratefully. "That would be nice."

The maestro smiled sadly. "Why don't you let me take you home to Genoa City?"

Leslie gripped his arm in a fervent protest. "Please, Maestro, not that."

"But, why?"

She turned away, devastated. Everything was lost. Everything. And now he wanted her to go home—a failure. "I don't want my family to know," she told him in a choked voice.

"Your family loves you," the maestro argued. "They'll understand."

"No," Leslie insisted. Tears were slowly falling down her cheeks now. "I can't face them. I'm too ashamed. Too . . . tired."

"But what will you do?"

She pulled a handkerchief out of her drawer and blew her nose. "Go away some place and rest."

The maestro frowned. "Where?"

"Please . . . I don't know. I'll try to think of some place." All she wanted at that moment was to be left alone. Maestro Fautsch was being wonderful, but she had to get away from him, away from everyone who even vaguely knew Leslie Brooks. She was such a fool! How could she ever face anyone after being such a fool?

"I am not sure you should be alone," the maestro replied uncertainly.

She clenched her fists. She had to hold on. Convince him. "I can handle it," she told him.

"The concert in Boston is only a week away." His voice became very gentle. "Do you want me to find a replacement for you?"

"No! Please!" She knew what another canceled concert could mean for him, for her, for everyone connected with the Mid-America Symphony. "I'll be all right," she assured him, her voice a little stronger now.

"Then you will meet the company in Boston?"

"Yes."

He studied her for a long time before he finally gave in. "Very well, Leslie," he told her at last. "But I hope I am not making a terrible mistake."

After he left her suite, she was able to hold herself together long enough to call Genoa City and tell her parents she wouldn't be coming home before the Boston concert.

"I thought I'd go to New York for a few days with some friends from the orchestra," she said, mustering up all the strength left in her ravaged body to make her voice appear light and casual. She didn't tell them what had happened at the theater a couple of hours ago or that the reason she was going to New York was because she would find anonymity there, could hide there.

"Have a wonderful time, honey," Stuart told her. "Glad you could take a few days off."

She started to break again while she was packing. She concentrated hard on getting everything into her suitcase, but somehow things kept falling out of her

hand. Bottles rolled across the floor, hairpins scattered.
She did the best she could. It didn't matter anyway, she
reminded herself. Nothing mattered now.

She was dimly aware of the late-night plane ride
and the taxi ride from La Guardia airport into the city.
She checked into a hotel she'd once heard somebody
mention, but once in her room, she found she couldn't
stay there. The voices were in her head again, more
ruthless and cruel than ever. And it wasn't only Lorie
she heard this time. Between her sister's taunts, between
the words "Brad and me," she heard Brad's voice
mocking her, laughing at her.

Did you really think I'd come to Detroit to see
your dumb concert? she thought she heard Brad saying.
Did you think I'd ever want to see you again after what
you wrote in that letter? How could you possibly think
I could have any feeling for you, Leslie? It's Lorie I
love. It's Lorie . . . Lorie . . . Lorie. . . .

She couldn't remember actually hearing him say
those things on the phone, but he was saying them now
and she knew she had to get out of there. She had to get
out of the room where the voices were. Grabbing her
purse, she hurried out of the room and flew down the
fire stairs, not even bothering to wait for the elevator.
It was raining outside, but that didn't matter. She
didn't even feel it pounding on her face as she walked
dazedly through the streets, not knowing—or caring
—where she was going.

And then she was in a park and it was dark, and a
man, a horrible, leering man, was telling her she
shouldn't be alone and trying to get her to go to his
pad with him. She didn't even answer him, just sat
on the bench with her makeup running down her face
in grotesque, orange streaks and her hair a wet tangle
around her shoulders. Finally, the man gave up and
left.

But then there was another man. No, not a man
—just a man's hand that suddenly flashed out from
the bushes and grabbed her purse, which was lying next
to her on the bench. She stared almost uncomprehend-

ingly as the purse was lifted up and snatched into the darkness. She heard the sound of footsteps running away. My purse, she thought dully. They've stolen my purse.

And then the whole horror of everything that had happened in the last five hours closed in on her and she found herself screaming wildly into the night.

"Will someone help me? Will someone help me? I need . . ." She was choking now, gasping for breath. "I need someone . . . someone to . . . help me. Will someone . . . anyone . . . help me. Please . . . I need someone. Anyone . . . please . . ."

Her last dim memory was of a policeman who took her arm and said something about a hospital.

11

"Any word from Leslie?" Brad asked Lorie. They were sitting in her apartment, relaxing after the beautiful dinner she'd fixed him, having cordials and listening to soft music. He guessed it was the music that made him think of Les. He still hadn't heard a word from her, and the Detroit concert had been almost a week ago.

"No," Lorie replied.

"Know where she's staying in New York?" He'd been surprised when Stuart told him she'd decided to go to New York instead of coming home to rest before the Boston concert.

Lorie looked at him with annoyance. "You're the most exasperating man, Brad Eliot," she declared grumpily.

He frowned. "How's that?"

"I go to all this trouble to create a mood—and all you have to talk about is my sister."

Brad ran a soothing hand down her back. "Just wanted to know how she was doing."

"Why are you so concerned about Les all the time?" Lorie's pretty nose was obviously very much out of joint.

"Didn't know I was," Brad told her truthfully.

Lorie looked at him sideways. "Sure you're not in love with her?"

"Lorie . . ." Brad sighed wearily. "I asked a simple question."

"For your information," she retorted, "Les is

probably living it up right now. Maybe even out on a fantastic date."

Brad gave her a concilatory kiss on the cheek. "I certainly hope so," he replied, nuzzling her neck.

She let her body rest against his for a moment, and then she pulled away and jumped up from the sofa. "Remember when I asked you to come over and I told you I had two surprises for you?" she asked, the irritability suddenly replaced by gay expectancy.

"I remember."

She flashed a triumphant look. "Ready for the first one?"

When he nodded, smiling at her enthusiasm, she went to her desk and picked up the sheaf of typewritten pages piled atop it. "My book," she announced, placing it carefully in his lap. "It's finished."

"Well!" Brad riffled quickly through the thick manuscript. "This is a surprise."

"Pleased with me?" Lorie asked, sounding like a little girl who's just brought home a straight-A report card.

"Very," he told her.

"You didn't really think I could do it, did you?"

Brad met her challenging eyes. "I think you can do anything you set your mind on, Lauralee Brooks."

Her expression grew softer then, and she sank back down next to him on the sofa. "You're the only one who encourages me," she said, bestowing a soft kiss on his cheek.

"Come on, Lorie," he chided. "That's not really true."

"It's true, Brad."

"Your family—"

She interrupted bitterly. "Their encouragement was all for Leslie. I had to find my own way."

"Be that as it may," Brad said, "you've found it now."

"I can't wait to get it into the hands of a publisher!" Bursting with excitement, she turned to him eagerly, her whole face aglow. "Oh, Brad, it's got to sell. I want that more than anything in the world."

"I hope," he said sincerely, "you get what you want." Then, putting the book aside, he turned to her again. "You said *two* surprises."

Lorie nodded and turned to him purposefully. "There's a possibility," she told him evenly, showing neither enthusiasm nor remorse, "I may be pregnant."

He stared at her. Pregnant? It was the last thing he'd expected to hear from a sophisticated gal like Lorie. Was she telling the truth? Or was she just trying to stir up a little excitement now that she didn't have her book to keep her occupied?

"Hey—did you hear me?" she pressed, thrown by his enigmatic silence.

"Uhh hmmm."

"I told you I may be pregnant. And if I am—what then, Mr. Eliot?"

He studied her face, searching for a clue as to what might be going on behind it. "We're not playing games now?" he queried.

"No."

"You've heard about the pill."

She laughed. "Gobble them like candy."

"Yet," Brad mused, "you *may* be pregnant."

Lorie looked at him a little guiltily. "It's nervous time, yes."

"How late are you?"

"About a week."

"I take it you're not usually irregular."

She was amused by his interrogation. "No, Doctor," she told him with exaggerated seriousness.

"But sometimes," he pressed, still not smiling.

"Very rarely."

"You seem casual enough about it." He remembered another girl— But no. That was one of the things he had to forget.

"What else?" she asked lightly. "Climbing the walls won't change anything, will it? Besides"—she cuddled up against him—"I'm much too happy to let *anything* bother me. Freshen your drink?"

"No, thanks."

She put her head on his shoulder and gazed out into the center of the room. "You still haven't answered me," she reminded him. "If I am—what then?"

"I don't know," Brad replied. "You tell me."

"Well, let's see now." She pursed her lips as if deep in thought. "There really aren't that many alternatives, are there?"

"No," he agreed, "there aren't."

"I suppose I could always spend a day or two in the hospital."

He suspected she was trying to get a rise out of him. Women usually thought that if they threatened abortion the man would be thunderstruck. "I wouldn't rush into anything," he answered mildly.

She pulled away from him so she could look into his face. "Meaning?" she asked carefully.

He shrugged. "A week late. I wouldn't panic."

She turned away and reached for her drink. "I must say you're being very casual about it, too."

He looked at her levelly. "Still think it's a put-on."

"Uh-uh," she said firmly. "Sorry."

"Then—it looks like we'll just have to wait it out."

Lorie nodded and was still for a moment. Then a wistful smile crossed her face. "Makes you wonder . . ." she said pensively.

"What?"

"What a child of ours would look like."

He frowned. This was certainly unexpected talk. "You ready for children?" he asked her.

She laughed. "The thought, Mr. Eliot, boggles my mind."

He breathed a little easier. This was the same old Lorie talking. "Any more than you're ready for marriage," he observed dryly.

"What about you?"

Brad was taken aback. "What about me?"

"And marriage." Lorie was casual, but she obviously expected a straight answer.

He shook his head uncertainly. "Someday, I suppose."

"That's the way I feel. Someday. Unless—" She broke off.

"What?" He knew she was baiting him, but he couldn't help being curious about what she was thinking.

"If I thought we loved each other . . ." She looked at him searchingly. "Do we, Brad?"

Love? Love Lorie? What kind of a question was that? What they had was a just-for-laughs thing—they'd agreed on that at the beginning. And now here she was, breaking all the rules and not only telling him she might be pregnant, but also asking him if they loved each other.

"I'm not sure what I feel," he said, trying to sidestep the whole thing. In a way, that was true. Perhaps Lorie was more right for him than he'd first thought.

She moved close to him again, her delicate perfume teasing his nostrils, her soft body feeling warm and inviting beneath her fuzzy sweater and soft wool pants. "Then suppose," she said seductively, planting dozens of tiny kisses on his face, "we both find out."

As her lips found his, his arms went around her and his answer was lost in the depth of their all-encompassing kiss.

Stuart Brooks was worried. Well, not worried, really, but concern for his eldest daughter was niggling persistently at the back of his mind. It had been five days since Les had called from Detroit to say she was going to spend some time in New York, and neither he nor anyone else in the family had heard from her since.

Peg, whose idea of New York was a continuous round of nightclubs and parties, had suggested her sister was having such a "ball" she hadn't had time to write or call. But Stuart didn't think that was it. If it had been Lorie who had gone off, yes. Lorie could go to a strange city, not knowing anybody, and become the belle of the place within twenty-four hours. He could see Lorie dancing till dawn, sleeping till noon, lunching at some elegant "in" restaurant, and never even remembering she had a family that might be concerned about her and wondering how she was doing. But not Leslie. Leslie had her feet on the ground, she'd never gone in for night life, and she hated being around strangers, even if they were handsome young men. And, he reflected with certainty, she was very close to her family. It just wasn't like her not to check in with them.

Of course, he reminded himself, he had no real reason to worry. If something were wrong, if there'd been an accident, he would have heard. Obviously the girl was just too busy shopping or attending concerts or whatever to think of phoning. But just to ease his mind a bit, he'd placed a call to Maestro Fautsch in Boston, to try and learn whether Leslie had been in touch with him and when she'd be arriving in Boston to prepare for the concert there. The maestro hadn't been in, but the hotel clerk had promised to give him the message Stuart left to return his call.

"Any word from Leslie yet?" Jennifer asked him when she arrived home from her community-club meeting.

"No," he told her, trying hard not to show his concern. He knew she was worried too, and he didn't want to make it worse for her.

"I just don't understand it," she said, her lovely brow wrinkling unhappily.

"I called Maestro Fautsch in Boston, but he was away from his hotel. I left word for him to call me as soon as he gets back."

Jennifer sank into a chair and became pensive. "Maybe Lorie has a point," she told him, almost abstractedly.

"About what?"

"She thinks Leslie may have deliberately decided not to get in touch with us this week."

Stuart frowned. "Why would she decide that?"

"To show her independence. Prove to herself she could really be on her own."

Stuart shook his head. It was logical—but it wasn't Leslie. "She'd know it would worry us," he argued, "not to hear from her at all."

Jennifer lifted her hands in an expression of doubt. "Lorie thinks Les decided it was time to cut the cord."

"If it were Lorie," Stuart told her, still refusing to accept it, "I'd buy it. But Les? I don't know—"

He was interrupted by the ringing of the phone, and he stepped quickly over to answer it.

"Hello?"

"Mr. Brooks?"

He couldn't fail to recognize the charming little Viennese accent. "Yes, Maestro," he said, already feeling more relieved. "Thanks for returning my call."

"Your call?" the maestro repeated.

"I left a message at your hotel."

The maestro sounded surprised. "I'm phoning from the concert hall to ask you if Leslie left for Boston yet."

So. Maestro Fautsch didn't know where she was either. "We haven't heard from her," Stuart told him, his agitation increasing.

"Not at all?" There was definite worry in the older man's voice.

"Not since she left for New York with some of her musician friends."

There was a long silence at the other end of the phone. Then "Leslie went to New York alone, Mr. Brooks."

"You're sure of that?" The dismay on his face caused Jennifer to rise and come to stand beside him, next to the phone.

"She was too ashamed to face anyone after what happened," the maestro said. Apparently, Stuart real-

ized, he was referring to something he and Jen should
have known about.

"What are you talking about?" Stuart asked, genuinely alarmed now. What could have happened to
make her ashamed?

There was a long pause before the maestro finally
spoke. "Then you don't know what happened in Detroit."

"We don't know anything!" His ominous excla-
mation caused Jennifer to grip his arm in fear.

"Leslie . . ." Realizing he was breeching a confidence, the maestro proceeded reluctantly. "Leslie
broke down in the middle of her solo."

"Was she ill?" Stuart asked quickly.

The maestro's voice was low. "Not ill."

"Then, for God's sake, what?"

"She was emotionally upset."

Emotionally upset? Leslie? Who not two weeks
ago had had the greatest triumph of her life? "From
what?" he asked, incredulous.

"I could learn very little from her," the maestro said apologetically. "Only that she was expecting
a man at the concert who did not appear."

This hit Stuart like a bolt of lightning. A man
was the last thing he expected to cause Leslie troubles.
"What man?" he asked, his confusion almost as great
as his anxiety.

"She did not tell me. But later, when I took her
back to her hotel, she said it was a phone call that
caused the upset."

"What phone call?" He felt as if they were speaking different languages now. It was all so unexpected, so
unlike Leslie.

"She refused to tell me. But it put her in a terrible
state."

"And we've been sitting here," Stuart said, shaking his head at the irony of it all, "thinking she was
having a good time vacationing in New York."

"The newspapers in Detroit were kind," the maes-

tro told him. "They published nothing about her breakdown for fear of hurting her career."

"I'm not thinking about her career right now,"
Stuart snapped. His concern was making him irritable.
"I'm concerned about my daughter's well-being."

"I'm waiting for her arrival here," Maestro
Fautsch said, trying to soothe him a little. "She prom-
ised when she left she would get to Boston tonight.
I'm sure she will."

"Will you have her call us the minute she ar-
rives?" Stuart knew neither he nor Jen would have a
moment's rest until they heard her voice.

"Of course I will, Mr. Brooks. Immediately."

When he hung up the phone, he told Jen what
Maestro Fautsch had said about the breakdown.

"And it was because of a man?" Jen asked in
bewilderment.

"Maestro Fautsch said it also had something to
do with a phone call."

"Stuart . . ." Jennifer's blue eyes were dark with
fear. "I'm worried that something terrible has happened
to Leslie."

He put a comforting arm around her trembling
shoulders. "Just hold on, darling," he begged her.
"Whatever it was, Leslie will tell us about it herself
when she calls."

Together, they sat on the sofa and waited for the
phone to ring. But the night crept by and there was
no word from her.

12

Manhattan Psychiatric Hospital was something of a New York embarrassment, rather like the Manhattan House of Detention or certain streets in Harlem. Once the leading psychiatric hospital in the country, it had long since been bypassed by the swift passage of time. Other, newer, more up-to-date hospitals had been built in the city; funds for Manhattan Psychiatric had become hard to come by; staff had dwindled due to poor salaries and long hours; overcrowding had become a serious problem.

Sometimes I wonder whether we can really be of help to our patients under these conditions, Dr. Malcolmson, the hospital's chief psychiatrist, thought to himself as he studied the file of the newest admittance, a young woman known only by the name of Jane Doe. Jane had been brought to the hospital nearly a week ago by a policeman who had found her wandering in Central Park in the middle of the night, not seeming to know who or where she was. Dr. Malcolmson had seen her the following morning, and like the policeman and the admitting clerk, he had been able to get little out of her. Apparently her purse had been stolen in the park, which accounted for the lack of identification on her, and although he felt that she was not actually suffering from amnesia, she offered no information to clear up the mystery surrounding her.

"Patient very depressed," Dr. Malcolmson had noted in her file after that first session. "Despondent.

106

Well oriented. Knows where she is and who she is, but is too depressed to talk. She denies pregnancy but has run away from home. Unhappy affair with boyfriend."

He had prescribed mild tranquilizers to allay the anxiety, and had had no choice but to put her in Ward A, where she had to share a room with three other tortured shells of human beings.

Jane Doe didn't really belong in that room, he thought resentfully as he went over his notes on their subsequent sessions. Right now, her depression was treatable. With proper care, she could be out of here and on an outpatient therapy program in a matter of weeks. But the longer she stayed at Manhattan Psychiatric, cooped up in a dreary, barred room with three poor souls whose sanity was all but gone, the more she would be likely to sink into an insanity of her own.

If only he could find out who she was! She was obviously someone of substance. Although the hospital had removed the clothes she was wearing when she was admitted and had given her a drab, shapeless smock, although she had not been allowed to use cosmetics or beauty aids since she had been here, she had an air of refinement about her that couldn't be ignored.

The last time he had seen her she had managed to talk a little, though still refusing to give her name. She said she wanted to leave—not go home (she seemed to have some deep fear of returning to her family), but to leave the hospital and go off someplace by herself. That was a good sign, he thought. Maybe in a few more days she'd want to leave so badly she *would* agree to his notifying her family to come and take her home. Also, there had been something about a sister that seemed to disturb her. He'd asked her whether she had any brothers or sisters, and at the word "sisters," she suddenly looked shocked and tears had sprung to her eyes.

"Do you want to talk about your sisters?" he had asked her. "It might make you feel better to talk about them."

She had come close to breaking down then, shaking her head and crying. "No . . . no . . . no. . . ."

"I guess you don't feel like talking about your problems today," he had said soothingly, pressing the buzzer that would alert the attendant to come and take her away. "We'll try again tomorrow."

Oh well, he thought now, closing the file and reaching for one marked Wanda Grazenka. He was doing all he could with her. Perhaps it would all work out better than he imagined.

"Doctor?" His secretary, Miss Warner, had poked her head in the door and was calling to him softly.

"Yes, Miss Warner?"

"One of the attendants would like to see you. She says it's urgent."

Usually Dr. Malcomson didn't like to be disturbed by hospital attendants, but Wanda's file could wait for a minute or two, so he told her to show the woman in.

The attendant was Miss Trendholm; not topnotch, actually, but probably more conscientious than most of the help Manhattan Psychiatric got these days.

"Come in, Miss Trendholm," he told her pleasantly. "What can I do for you?"

The woman held out a small piece of paper. When he took it, he realized it was a newspaper clipping. "It's from a Boston newspaper," the attendant explained. "Miss Kelly's from there. She was reading it and saw this."

He studied it. It was a notice about a concert that would take place in Boston tomorrow night.

"Look at the picture," Miss Trendholm urged him.

It was a picture of a pretty girl, the soloist with the symphony orchestra, the clipping said.

"Don't you think it looks vaguely like Jane?"

He squinted to get a better perspective. "It does, a little," he agreed. He read the caption aloud. "Miss Leslie Brooks, brilliant young piano virtuoso, opening in Boston tomorrow night as soloist with Mid-America Symphony Orchestra." He frowned. "Think it's possible that could be our Jane?" Without replying, Dr. Malcolmson continued reading the text. "Daughter of Stuart Brooks, owner and publisher of the Genoa City *Chronicle*."

"Sure looks a lot different than that now." Miss Trendholm had come over to his side of the desk and was peering at the picture over his shoulder.

"If it's the same girl," he told her.

"There is a chance."

He nodded. "There's a resemblance all right."

Miss Trendholm shook her head sadly. "I thought there was something different about that girl when they first brought her in."

Dr. Malcolmson continued to stare at the picture. As the attendant had pointed out, Leslie Brooks was a lot more vibrant and glamorous-looking than Jane Doe —but there *was* something, something about her bone structure and features that were undeniably similiar.

"It just might possibly be," he mused thoughtfully.

"I hope so. I feel so sorry for Jane."

"It's certainly worth a call to Genoa City. Thank you, Miss Trendholm, for bringing this to my attention."

When she'd left, he picked up the phone and asked Miss Warner to place a call to a Mr. or Mrs. Stuart Brooks in Genoa City. He held on while the secretary got the number from Information and had the operator complete the call. A man answered the ring in the Brooks home.

"Mr. Stuart Brooks?" Dr. Malcolmson asked.

"Yes, this is he."

"I'm Dr. Malcolmson, from the Manhattan Psychiatric Hospital in New York City."

There was a tiny moment of silence at the other end, as if Brooks had been shocked by the words. "Yes, Dr. Malcolmson?" he said warily.

"I want to ask you what may seem like a peculiar question, Mr. Brooks."

"Yes? Go ahead."

Malcomson drew a breath. Something . . . something foreboding in the man's manner made him think he was on the right track. "How long has it been since you heard from your daughter Leslie?" he asked carefully.

Again, he could feel the man's shock. "A week," Stuart replied.

"Is it possible she might be in New York?"

"Yes. The last we heard, she was there. But she's due in Boston tonight."

"I see," Malcolmson said thoughtfully.

"Do you have some news about her?"

"There's a possibility I may have. I'm not sure. We have a young woman patient here who was brought in a week ago suffering from a deep depression."

"Why do you think she may be my daughter?" Brooks sounded quietly frantic, like a man who was hoping when he knew all hope was gone.

"She refuses to tell us her name or anything about her background."

"Then why . . .?"

"One of the attendants brought a Boston newspaper to my attention. There's a picture of your daughter in it. And we think it bears some resemblance to this patient."

He could hear Brooks suck in his breath. "Good God!"

"I can't be sure," Malcolmson cautioned him. "But it is a possibility that our patient is your daughter. You, of course, could make a positive identification."

Brooks' answer was immediate. He didn't even have to stop and think. "I'll be in New York on the next plane," he said briskly.

When Malcolmson hung up the phone, he felt a deep sense of relief. It was a shot in the dark—but he may have helped Jane Doe after all.

Thank God, Stuart thought when he walked into the ward and saw her for the first time, that Jen isn't here to see this. She'd wanted to come, had been almost inconsolable when he'd insisted on coming to New York without her, but he was so afraid of what he might find, he just had to save her as much pain as he possibly could. And this, he thought, his stomach twisting sickeningly, would have just about killed her.

At first he hadn't even recognized the young woman who sat on her cot, calmly reading the Twenty-third Psalm aloud from an old, worn Bible. Her long, tangled hair was partially covering her face and she was all hunched over, like a woman three times her age. She was surrounded by three other patients, all of whom looked at him curiously as he came into the ward with Dr. Malcolmson. A small, wizened old woman gestured to a rag doll lying on another cot and said to him graciously, "I believe you know my baby son, Joey."

Stuart had nodded to her pityingly and stared at the young woman with the Bible.

"She's not my daughter," he'd told the doctor with enormous relief.

"Are you certain of that?" The doctor guided him closer, so he could get an unobstructed view.

As soon as he saw the face behind the hair, he knew. His whole body seemed to stop functioning as the shock of seeing her this way set in. He could neither speak nor move. He could only stand where he was and gaze at her, incredulous and in horror.

She stopped reading, but did not look at him. Her eyes focused somewhere in space. They were haunted, full of deep pain.

"Leslie," he said, finding his voice at last and taking a cautious step toward her. "Leslie, sweetheart, it's Dad."

She didn't speak, didn't even look up. Agonized, he went to her and tenderly brushed the tangled hair back from her face. "Honey, it's me. Look at me. It's Dad."

Although she remained silent, tears suddenly sprang into her haunted eyes. Seeing them, he gathered her into his arms and crooned to her as if she were a child. "Oh, dear God—Leslie, honey, it's me. You'll be all right now."

"Leslie, talk to me, say something to me," he begged as she held herself stiff and impassive in his arms.

"Your father's here," one of the women piped up helpfully. "Talk to him, Jane."

"I've come to take you home, honey," Stuart said gently.

"No!" He looked back sharply as one of the other women made a loud protest. She was younger than the other two, dark and mannish looking. Her brooding eyes fixed on Leslie possessively. "Don't take her away from me," she commanded angrily. "I like her. She's so pretty. So pretty . . . my Jane. . . ."

Suddenly the woman with the rag doll approached Stuart. "I believe we met at the Riverview Bridge Club last week," she said, smiling at him companionably.

Stuart stared at her, not knowing how to answer.

"Don't you remember?" she persisted. "We were partners."

"Wanda," the "helpful" woman intervened, "your baby's crying."

Wanda sighed. "Oh dear," she said to Stuart, "you'll have to excuse me. Joey doesn't like me to leave him alone." She hurried to her cot and picked up her doll, cradling it in her arms and humming a little lullaby.

The horror of it all consumed Stuart. To think of Leslie—here—with these women!

"Please, Leslie," he begged, himself close to tears now. "For the love of God, look at me! Look at me! Don't you know your father?" He turned to Dr. Malcolmson despairingly. "Does she recognize me?" he asked.

The doctor nodded. "She recognizes you. But her trauma is forcing her to reject you. She's convinced herself she's not worthy of having a family."

"Leslie," Stuart said, urgently trying to get through to her, "whatever's happened, we all love you and want you back with us. Honey, I want to take you home. Do you hear me?"

If she did, she gave no sign. Finally Dr. Malcolmson suggested returning to his office to decide what to do and where to go from there.

"She's suffering from a severe depression," Malcolmson told him. "In a case like this, she believes she isn't worthy of your love. That's why she rejects you."

"She's so thin," Stuart said dazedly. "So pale. A shadow of the girl she was."

The doctor nodded in understanding. "You have to expect physical side effects with emotional upheaval like this."

"What could have done this to her?"

"It's too early to have any definite answers, Mr. Brooks. But part of her problem is what you told me earlier about the concert in Detroit. The breakdown on the stage was such an overwhelming humiliation, it continues to haunt her."

"I wish to God now that I'd never encouraged her to play the piano," Stuart muttered bitterly.

"I don't think," the doctor said frankly, "her music is our answer. There is something else—or someone else." When Stuart said nothing, merely looked at him utterly baffled, he became very earnest. "I hope you can find a way to persuade her to leave here with you. We do our best, but we're vastly overcrowded and understaffed, like all public hospitals. She'd be much better off in a private hospital, close to her own home. However," he added quickly, "it could cause great damage if you force her to leave against her wishes."

"Would it be possible," Stuart asked, "for me to talk to my daughter alone? Just the two of us?" He couldn't believe she would have to be *forced* to leave.

"Yes," Dr. Malcolmson agreed. "I'll bring her here to you."

While the doctor was gone, he placed a call to Jen in Genoa City. Knowing it would be unfair to keep the truth from her, he told her the whole story, eliminating only the dreadful conditions of the hospital and the circumstances under which Leslie was forced to live.

"When are you bringing her home?" Jen asked, obviously holding on to herself very tight to keep from crying.

"Jen," Stuart replied gently, "she doesn't want to come home. In fact, she doesn't even want to recognize me as her father."

"I want to talk to her," Jen said, a little sob in her voice now.

"Yes," he agreed. "That would be good."

"I want our daughter home."

"Yes, darling, God knows we both want that."

He turned toward the door as Dr. Malcolmson led Leslie into his office. She started at Stuart blankly. "She's here," he said to Jennifer. "Hold on."

He put the receiver down on Dr. Malcolmson's desk and went over to Les. "Leslie, darling," he beseeched her, "please, let me take you home. Back to Genoa City."

Leslie shrank away from him. She opened her mouth as if to speak, but no words came out. "Afraid," she finally managed to whisper.

"You don't have to be afraid, my darling. There's a lovely, quiet hospital just outside of Genoa City. I want to take you there, honey." Dr. Malcolmson's suggestion of a private hospital had reminded him of Fairview. It was close to home, and it had an impressive reputation.

Leslie shook her head. "Don't . . . know . . ."

"You'll be able to have a nice room, all by yourself, with no one to bother you. You'll get better care there, sweetheart. It's not overcrowded and understaffed like this place. And your mother and I will be able to see you as often as you want us." He put an arm around her and pulled her close. "Please, darling, I beg of you, let me take you there. Don't ask me to leave you here. I can't. It would break my heart."

She looked at him, tears streaming down her face once more. Suddenly, he remembered Jen. "Look," he said, gently guiding her to Dr. Malcolmson's desk where the telephone lay, "here's someone who wants to talk to you." He spoke into the mouthpiece. "I'm putting Leslie on."

He held the receiver to her ear, and she listened wordlessly as her mother echoed his pleas. "Don't . . . don't want anyone to know," she said once. "Not . . . *anyone.*"

As her face contorted in pain, he realized her mother must be crying. "Mom?" she said at last, showing, as Dr. Malcolmson pointed out to Stuart later, the first signs of concern for anyone since she'd been there, "Mom . . . don't . . . please . . . don't. . . ." She listened again, putting a hand to her face to brush back her tears. "Yes," she whispered at last, to her father's enormous relief. "Yes . . . I'll . . ." As Stuart rushed to embrace her, she broke into great racking sobs. "Oh, Mom," she choked. "Dad . . . Mom . . . Dad . . ."

13

For Lorie, life had never been more exciting. Funny, she mused as she mixed the martinis she'd soon be sharing with Brad, it was less than six months ago that I was thinking of leaving Genoa City and moving to Chicago or New York. I thought if I stuck around here, nothing would ever happen to me and I'd simply rot away.

But since then, just about *everything* had happened to her—everything she wanted, anyway. A publisher—a big publisher in New York—was very interested in her book, and she'd know soon whether she was going to be getting a contract. And if she didn't, well, the fact that this house was so interested proved the book was good, and the next house she took it to would be sure to want it.

And her love life was positively dazzling! Who'd've thought a man like Brad Eliot could be found in Genoa City, she thought, smiling, giving the martinis a gentle stir and placing the glass pitcher in the refrigerator. Of course, she knew he wasn't there because he wanted to be. She hadn't gotten to the bottom of that business about the accident yet, but she was sure he had run away from something and had settled in Genoa City because of the anonymity he'd been able to find there. But that's my good luck, she told herself happily. If Brad hadn't been running away . . . if the accident hadn't happened . . . if Leslie hadn't . . .

116

Leslie. There it was again. The one name that almost managed to prick her beautiful balloon. Why should she feel guilty about Leslie? Sure, Les had seen Brad first. But she hadn't been woman enough to attract him. Surely she, Lorie, couldn't be held responsible for *that*, could she? As for that dumb business about the letter . . . well, Les should never have written such a thing in the first place. Brad was unprepared for a declaration of her love, he'd have been embarrassed by it. The way Lorie saw it, she'd saved everyone a lot of discomfort.

She glanced at the clock. Quarter to seven. He'd be there any minute now. She was even more eager to see him tonight than usual because she was determined to pursue the conversation they'd had at the office this morning. They'd been working side by side, correcting galleys, and Lorie, overcome by the nearness of him, had suddenly burst out with a confession.

"Never thought it would happen to me," she'd said, careful to keep her voice low and her eyes on the galleys, "but I think I'm falling in love with you, Brad Eliot."

She hadn't been able to see the expression on his face, but his voice had been a little choked when he said, "Suppose we talk about that later."

He's got to be in love with me, too! she thought as she gave herself a final critical inspection in the full-length foyer mirror. I know he thinks I'm frivolous and spoiled—but there's so much more to me beneath the surface, and he knows that, too. Whatever may have happened to Brad in the past, however he may have felt about Barbara Anderson—or even Leslie—I'm the right woman for him now.

In a way, she'd almost been disappointed when her pregnancy scare had turned out to be a false alarm. If she'd been carrying his child, he might have realized she was the right woman a lot sooner. Now she'd have to find another way. But she'd do it—she had no doubt of that.

She smoothed her hair as the doorbell rang, and

rushed to answer it. "Hi, darling," she greeted, throwing her arms around his neck.

He hugged her. "Nice way to be welcomed," he said, grinning.

"Sit right down and relax. I have our cocktails all prepared."

While she was in the kitchen pouring the martinis, he called out from the living room, "Heard from Stuart?"

"I talk to him now and then." For some mysterious reason her father had been spending very little time at the paper lately. He said he was involved in some kind of business deal, but both Brad and Lorie thought it odd that he suddenly seemed to be neglecting the *Chronicle*.

"He dropped into the office for a minute after you left," Brad told her as she brought in the drinks and handed him a frosty glass. "Seemed troubled."

"About what?" Lorie took a sip of her drink and settled herself next to him on the sofa.

"Didn't say. But he really seemed depressed."

"Bet he's pleased with the way you've been handling things for him," Lorie said proudly.

Brad nodded. "Seems to be. By the way," he added, turning to her and bestowing a quick kiss on her forehead, "thanks for your help with the galleys this afternoon."

Lorie grinned at him. "Then you do remember? My help—and what I said to you?"

"Oh, yes."

"I was beginning to wonder if you heard me."

"Loud and clear," he assured her with an ironic smile.

"You were so businesslike," she chided impishly.

"With a half-hour to go before deadline, I didn't have much choice."

Lorie put her free hand up to his face and looked at him searchingly. "Brad," she said softly, "I meant what I said. I think I'm falling in love with you." She took a deep breath. "Never said that to a man before."

He met her eyes. "I believe you," he said quietly.

"Marriage has always been . . . well, unthinkable."

He smiled knowingly. "Live for the moment, and the rest be damned."

"Exactly," she admitted. "But now all that's changed. Just the thought—" She broke off, letting it hang.

"Of what?" Brad prodded.

"Of you with another woman. I couldn't stand to have that happen."

Brad looked at her curiously. "You say that as though there *is* another woman."

"No," she assured him quickly. "None that I know of." She studied him. "Any that you know of?"

He grinned. "No."

"Well, I don't want to risk it."

He pulled her closer. She felt so comfortable, so at home in his arms. "You've nothing to fear."

She smiled contentedly at his words, but after a moment she said with a little urgency in her voice, "Brad, this is no way to live. You in that dumb little furnished room, alone. And I'm tired of being alone."

He gave her a wry look. "If you're thinking of suggesting we live together, it won't work. In New York or Chicago, maybe, but not Genoa City."

She pursed her lips. "I wasn't thinking of 'living together.'"

Brad was suddenly very still. "Lorie," he said after a long, thoughtful moment, "how much do you know of me, really?"

She shrugged. "All I have to."

He nodded. "Which isn't very much. A man who came here without a past, trying to find a new life, a new world."

"And you've found a new life, made a new world for yourself."

"That's not enough, Lorie. It's no real basis for a marriage. At least it shouldn't be for you."

She frowned petulantly. "Because you're running away from the past," she said, impatient with him for coming up with such a flimsy excuse.

"A past I'm not willing to share with anyone."

She was thoughtful for a moment. Should she tell him? Confess she'd learned certain things about his past weeks ago in Chicago? Yes, she decided, she *had* to tell him. There was no other way. "Brad," she began carefully, taking his hand and holding it tight, "you won't have to. Because . . . I already know."

A little glint of fear flashed in his eyes. "Know what?"

She took a deep breath. Too late to back out now. "That you're a doctor."

He said nothing for a long time, merely sat staring off into space, as if the whole thing were too much for him to comprehend. Finally, he turned to her and asked quietly, "How long have you known?"

"Over a month."

"How did you find out?"

She lowered her eyes. "By doing something I had no right to do. The night I came to your room, to bring you my book—remember?"

He kept his eyes on her. "I remember."

"You were in the shower. I saw your billfold on the dresser." She swallowed hard. What was he thinking? Was he hating her at this moment? "It was horrible of me," she went on nervously, "but I was already interested in you. I wanted to see if I could find out something about you." She looked up at him with a guilty little smile. "You can tell so much from a woman's purse or a man's billfold."

He heaved a sigh of understanding. "And you hit pay dirt."

"I found the teletype—the wire photo of you. I found out you were a doctor, a Chicago neurosurgeon and psychiatrist, and that everyone thought you were dead." She stopped and waited for him to say something, but there was no reaction, nothing. "Do you hate me for finding out this way?" she asked weakly.

He didn't look at her, but seemed to be staring, unseeing, into space. "You've known all this time." It wasn't an answer to her question, it was an almost incredulous musing.

"Yes, Brad," she replied. "All this time. And never once a word to anyone." She was aware, of course, that that wasn't quite true. She *had* talked to Barbara Anderson about him. But for the moment, she decided, that had best be left unsaid. When he was silent, she tried to draw him out, thinking that talking about what happened would somehow ease the pain. "The teletype said it was a car accident, that the car burned up. Who was the man who was killed? The man everyone believed was you?"

He was quiet for another minute, then he rose from the sofa and began to pace the room, deeply caught up in the past he had long since put in the carefully walled-off recesses of his mind.

"I was driving," he said slowly, laboriously. "I stopped at a roadside restaurant for something to eat. A man watched me when I took out my wallet to pay my bill." He stopped and shook his head. "Didn't think anything about it at the time. But, later, after I got back in my car and was driving for a while—" His face clouded. "He'd been in the back seat all along. Suddenly he rose up behind me and put a gun to the back of my head. It felt cold . . . and deadly.

"He told me to pull over and get out of the car. He wanted my wallet . . . my watch . . . even my cuff links. I gave them to him, of course"—here he gave an ironic little laugh—"can't argue with a gun pointed at your head. But when he reached out to take them, I kind of lunged at him. But he was too quick for me. He hit me. Here." He put a hand up to the side of his head cautiously, as if it still hurt.

"The scalp wound Dad said you had when he saw you at Pierre's," Lorie said.

Brad nodded. "He knocked me out cold. When I woke up, he was gone. And so was my car." He took a deep, quavering breath. "The man who died had to be the mugger who knocked me out and drove off with my car."

"But why," Lorie wanted to know when the horror of the facts had settled in, "did you let everyone think you were dead? Why did you leave Chicago? Give up your practice?"

He stopped his pacing and looked at her, and an expression of deep pain crossed his face. "That's part of my past that I'm not ready to share with anyone," he said quietly.

"Not even with me, Brad?"

"With no one."

She rose from the sofa and took his hand tenderly. "I want to understand you in every way," she pleaded, her eyes glowing with emotion. "To do that, I have to understand your past." As he looked at her expressionlessly, she added urgently, terrified now that he would be unable to forgive what she had done, "Please, Brad, don't be upset or angry because I learned about your other life."

He turned away. "I don't know what I feel," he told her dully.

Lorie brought his hand, so lifeless in her grasp, to her lips and kissed it. "I feel closer to you than ever before," she whispered. "To me, it's very special, very precious to share your past with you. It's just between us. I'll never tell anyone. You can count on that."

"Can I?" he asked tonelessly.

"Don't you trust me, Brad?"

"I thought I did."

"Believe me, you can." She looked at him appealingly. "Our relationship has become very special to me. This could bring us even closer."

He offered a wan smile and shook his head. "It can't be the same between us now."

"It can be even better," she protested. "And if you want to forget your past—never speak of it again—that's all right with me, too. Whatever you want is what I want."

She released his hand and touched his face tenderly. "You mean so much to me, Brad. More than any man I've ever known." She kissed him gently on the lips, but he simply stood there, not responding. "Love me, Brad," she begged him. "Make love to me." She wound her arms around him and pressed herself against his body. Slowly, under her gentle prodding, his lifeless arms found their strength and returned her trembling embrace. And the next thing she knew, he was kissing her with more urgency than he had ever displayed in all the time they had been together.

Brad lay awake, thinking about it. So, his secret was out. Lorie knew that he was Dr. Bradley Eliot, neurosurgeon and psychiatrist, of Chicago, Illinois. Lorie knew that he was the man everyone from his past thought was dead.

Lorie. Her face flashed before his eyes the way it had looked last night: earnest, appealing, filled with love and compassion for him. What she'd done—opening his billfold like that—was unforgivable. And yet . . . He felt almost relieved that one other living soul knew the truth about him, that he could share at least part of the past that had been haunting him all these months.

Can I trust her? he asked himself, staring up at the shadowy ceiling. Or do I start running again, lose myself all over again? He shuddered at the thought. This new life of mine, it's been a good one. Another world I've found a place in. The past buried in that grave in Quincy. He heaved a sigh. Until tonight. And now? Do I leave what I've found here? To go . . . where? Or *can* I really trust Lorie?

He was torn in his feelings about her. The fact that she'd known for weeks and had said nothing . . . the fact that she wanted to marry him. He tossed in his bed. How do I feel about that? he asked himself, troubled. Lauralee Brooks. In love. With me.

Last night she had hinted at marriage; she had asked—no, begged—him to love her. And he had *made* love to her in return. But making love and loving

. . . it wasn't the same thing. How did he feel about her, really? She was a beautiful, exciting, extremely intelligent woman, the kind of woman many men looked for all their lives. Of course, he thought with a wry grin, she wasn't exactly your run-of-the-mill house-wife type. Spirited, willful, unpredictable, she'd be a handful for any man. But she was so-lovely . . . and she loved him.

It could be an end to all the loneliness, he thought solemnly. Becoming part of a family I've come to love and respect. And, he remembered with a pang of satisfaction, who have come to like and respect me. Even Jennifer Brooks had warmed up to him lately, seeing somehow that, whatever his past, he was not the ominous character she'd once imagined him to be.

Is it the answer? he wondered. He ran a hand across his perspiring brow as the thought of Lorie and her beauty returned. A strong sexual attraction—it's important, but is it all I feel? No. It's much more than that. It's also her needs, the feeling that I can help her. It's that same feeling, in a different way, I had with Leslie. Though, he reminded himself, it was simpler with Leslie—objective, impersonal. Maybe it could have been more, but Les had never wanted that, evident-ly doesn't ever want that kind of emotional commit-ment.

He sighed when he thought of Les. He still hadn't heard from her, not since she'd left for the Detroit concert. And then there had been Boston and, he thought, Philadelphia. He had sent her a wire wishing her well in Boston, but Western Union had phoned him back and said she couldn't be located. That had an-noyed him. The biggest thing to hit Boston in years, and Western Union couldn't find her! Well, he thought sincerely, his mind sending waves of good wishes to her through the night, I hope you have triumph after triumph. You have so much to give . . . your talent, your sweetness, the very goodness of you. I miss you, Les. And yet, he admitted, still addressing her in his mind, it was good for you to cut the cord. Reach out, stand secure on your own. If I helped you do that, I'm thankful.

But I still miss hearing from you.

Knowing he wouldn't be able to sleep this night, he rose from his bed and went over to gaze out the window. The familiar street below was quiet, but the sight of it warmed his heart. This was Genoa City, where he had come as a stranger. And he had done well here, had found a place for himself, had grown to love the town and its people. How could he leave a place he loved—for the second time?

Maybe it *is* the answer, he thought reflectively. Maybe Lorie is the answer.

The next day he asked her to marry him.

14

Fairview Hospital, some twenty miles outside Genoa City, looked more like a private estate than a sanatorium. The main building was, in fact, a reconverted Tudor mansion where the patients lived in quiet dignity among understated elegance. The public rooms, like the card room and the television room, were furnished primarily with antiques, and the bedrooms—each patient had his or her own—were airy and cheerful, with chintz curtains billowing at the windows and soft plush carpets covering the floors.

A far cry from that God-forsaken place in New York, Stuart thought as he swung his car out of the huge wrought-iron main gate and headed back to town. Every time he thought of that place and the way Leslie had looked when he'd first seen her there, he shuddered. And to think, she hadn't wanted to leave at first! The poor girl was so ashamed and humiliated by whatever had caused her breakdown that she hadn't wanted to go with her own father to a place that could give her the help she needed to get well.

Well, he told himself, she was at Fairview now —although, despite good care and the best doctors, her condition had improved very little. He'd come to see her every day since she'd been there (spending so little time at the office Brad Eliot was actually running the paper now), and each time she'd looked exactly the same; pale, haunted, a tortured shell of her beautiful former self. Dr. Berger had told him this morning that, unless Leslie opened up to him about what happened before that concert in Detroit, she might never get well. And Leslie simply refused to talk about it. She denied everything Maestro Fautsch had told Stuart about the minutes before the concert had begun; that she was waiting for a man, that there had been a telephone call, everything.

Stuart had tried himself, more than once, to get the information out of her, but Leslie had closed herself off from him, become cold and distant, and flatly denied that anything the maestro said was true.

The only real change either he or Jen had seen in her these last weeks was that she had at last agreed that her sisters could be told the truth about where she was. Until just the other day, she had insisted that they remain in the dark, that they think all was well with her, and that the reason they hadn't heard from her was she was so busy dashing from concert to concert she hadn't had a minute to write or call. But all the girls had been getting suspicious—they knew Les was too closely bound to the family to forsake them no matter *how* busy she was—and upon Stuart and Jen's gentle urging, Leslie had finally consented to their being told.

Chris had been told first—and she was understandably shocked. She'd insisted on going right out to Fairview to see her sister, and the two had had a touching reunion. Like Stuart and Jennifer, Chris had tried to get Les to open up about the man and the phone call, but glad as Les was to see her, her questions were to no avail.

Lorie and Peg had not been told as yet. Lorie was in New York on some mysterious mission she refused to talk about, and Jennifer and Stuart had decided they should tell Peg together, and the right moment had not arisen. They would probably tell her this evening, Stuart decided. He hoped to God it wouldn't be too painful for her. Peg, so bright-eyed and eager about life, was getting ready to graduate from high school. It should be a beautiful time for her. And she had to be told her adored big sister was in a mental hospital.

He arrived home to find her regaling her mother with the details of graduation rehearsals, demonstrating with mock seriousness the slow walk she would have to make to the strains of "Pomp and Circumstance," and describing how her mortarboard had been too big for her and fell down over her eyes until an observant teacher had suggested stuffing it with tissue paper.

"Gosh, I sure hope Les will be able to make it home in time for the ceremony," she said wistfully, when she'd given Stuart a welcoming hug and Jen had filled him in on the subject of their hilarious conversation. "It won't be the same without her."

Stuart's eyes met Jennifer's for a brief moment. "I talked to Les this afternoon," he said.

Peg's face brightened. "Did she say anything about coming home?"

"Jen," Stuart said quietly, "I think it's time to tell her."

"Tell me what?" Peg came over to him and cocked her head to one side.

He took her hand and held it. "Your mother and I have been forced to do a lot of pretending lately, Peg," he said gently.

Her pert face worked itself into a frown. "You know, I felt something funny was going on with you guys, the way you've been acting. But what's it got to do with Les?"

"It has everything to do with Les, honey," Jennifer told her.

"Well, what?"

Stuart took a deep, unhappy breath. "She's in the hospital, Peg."

"Hospital? Where? In Boston?" Peg's eyes grew round as saucers.

He looked at her steadily. "Here—in Fairview."

To his dismay the girl's whole body seemed to stiffen and then crumble, as if the shock were too much for her to bear. "But, that's a . . ." She broke off, unable to say the words.

"Yes, Peg," Stuart finished quietly, "Leslie had an

emotional breakdown in Detroit. She's suffering from a deep depression. But we're hopeful now that the doctors will be able to pull her out of it."

"But, why—" Peggy's voice cracked. She seemed near tears. "Why didn't you tell me?"

He patted her hand. "Leslie didn't want anyone to know."

"But . . . what happened? Everything was going so great for Les. Why would she break down?"

"We don't know."

"When the doctor finds out what caused it," Jennifer said, "he'll be able to find a way to help her."

Peggy stood stock still for a long moment. Tears had sprung to her eyes and were slowly trickling down her cheeks. She put up a hand to wipe them away and then, suddenly, she turned forcefully to her father. "Dad, I want to see her. Now. Tonight."

He was on the verge of telling her it was too late, that patients weren't allowed visitors after six o'clock, but the expression on her face told him she needed to see her sister right now more than she had ever needed anything before in her young life. "I'll call Dr. Berger," he said tersely.

A short time later, he, Jen, and Peg, with the doctor's permission, were admitted to the hospital and shown to Leslie's room by a kindly-looking nurse in a crisp white uniform. The door was open, and they could see Les stretched out on the bed, staring listlessly off into space. While Stuart and Jennifer lagged behind, Peg moved cautiously into the room and approached her sister.

"Les . . ." Her eyes were again filling with tears.

Leslie turned her head in surprise. "Peg," she said with real warmth. "Baby sister." She held out her arms and Peg fell into them, crying openly now.

"I've missed you so much, Les."

Gently, Les pulled out of the embrace and looked tenderly into her face. She touched one of the tears shining on Peg's cheek. "You mustn't cry for me, honey."

"It's . . . just that I'm glad to see you," Peg told her, trying valiantly to manage a smile. "I've been thinking about you so much lately—wanting to talk things over with you, the way I always have."

"I don't think I'd be very good at giving advice anymore, Peg," Les said, smiling sadly.

Peg buried her head in her breast. "Just seeing you is enough. Oh, Les, I love you!"

"And I love you, baby."

"Get well soon, Les, so you can come home." She raised her head and looked at her earnestly. "The house is so empty without you. Every time I come home I hope I'll hear the sound of your piano—that you'll be there." Her voice became a plea. "You've got to get better—real soon."

They embraced again, and then Peggy, ever the charmer, made an attempt to cheer her sister up. "Hey, so much has happened since you've been away," she said with the eagerness that, though forced at the moment, was so much a part of her personality. "I'm about to graduate . . . and Mark wanted to give me his pin but I wouldn't take it . . . and Brad and Lorie are engaged. . . ." She broke off breathlessly.

Leslie's face, which had reflected such delight when the chatter began, suddenly clouded.

"Brad and Lorie?" she asked, looking to her parents for confirmation.

"Yes, honey, it happened just the other day," Jennifer told her. "I guess Stuart forgot to mention it."

"He gave her a super ring!" Peg enthused. "Nothing so mundane as a diamond. It's a star sapphire!"

"I see." All the pleasure at seeing Peg seemed to have gone from her eyes, and she slumped back on her bed. "Look," she said tensely. "I'm glad you came, but I'm awfully tired all of a sudden. Do you think you could . . ."

"Of course, darling," Stuart answered. "We'll let you rest. Come, Peg."

Peg hesitated. "You'll let me come out here to see you again, Les?"

"Yes, honey," her sister assured her softly. "You can come whenever you want."

She was cradling her pillow and staring off into space when, reluctantly, they turned and trooped out the door.

Brad knew something was wrong, very wrong. And he was as certain as he'd ever been of anything in life that it had to do with Leslie. First there'd been that business about Western Union's not being able to locate her in Boston. He'd thought it was strange at the time, considering the fact that he'd sent the wire directly to the concert hall only a short time before she was due to begin her concert, but when they'd called back and he'd had to cancel it, he'd decided it must have just been a crazy mix-up.

But then Stuart had begun acting funny. He'd gone away unexpectedly on what he'd called a "business trip," at about the same time as the telegram fiasco, and since he'd returned to Genoa City, he'd put very little time in at the paper. Naturally, Brad had been glad for the opportunity to take on the new responsibility that had been put on his shoulders, but he sensed there was much more behind Stuart's absence than a business deal he was working on. The man was worried. It was all too plain.

Finally, just this morning, Brad had had a shock. He'd answered Stuart's phone and had taken a message for his boss from a Dr. Berger at Fairview Hospital. *Fairview*. With a message for Stuart. Slowly, purposefully, he began to fit the pieces of the puzzle together.

For a long time now he'd thought it strange that no one—not even her family—had heard from Les since she'd left Genoa City for the series of concerts beginning in Detroit. Several times he'd asked Lorie what she made of her sister's not writing or phoning, but she'd simply shrugged it off, saying, as she had said so many times before, that Les was undoubtedly enjoying her new life-style so much that she had no use for anyone as dull as members of the Brooks family of Genoa City. And when he broached the subject to Stuart, his boss had just said Les was probably busy and let it go at that.

But it wasn't right, none of it. Leslie was too close to her family to neglect them so completely. And now Stuart was worried and a doctor from Fairview Hospital wanted to talk to him. It all added up. Leslie —lovely, vulnerable, Leslie—was a patient at a place for the mentally ill.

But *was* she mentally ill? What could have happened to have caused her to be admitted to a place like Fairview? And had Lorie been hiding the truth from him—or was it possible that Les' sisters didn't know anything about it?

He was contemplating the meaning of it all when Stuart came through the bullpen on the way to his office.

"Stuart," Brad called out in surprise. "Didn't expect you so early."

"Just stopped by for a moment. How are things going?"

Brad shrugged. "Everything under control."

The older man nodded, pleased. "Looks like I don't have to worry about anything with you here, Brad."

Brad regarded him carefully. "I think you have enough on your mind without worrying about the office," he told him. Then he added purposefully, "Did you get the message from Dr. Berger? I asked your secretary to give it to you if you called in."

"Yes," Stuart replied, looking decidedly uncomfortable. "Thanks."

"He said he was from Fairview."

When Stuart said nothing, merely nodded and averted his eyes, Brad said bluntly, "I understand that's a private psychiatric hospital."

Stuart swallowed. "That's right."

Brad studied him for a long moment. Then he zeroed in on what he'd been thinking all morning. "That's where Leslie is, isn't it, Stuart?"

In the next moment Stuart's careful self-control was stripped away and he suddenly looked to Brad like an old, beaten, world-weary man. "Yes," he admitted quietly. "She's there."

"What happened to her?"

"She broke down emotionally in Detroit, in the middle of her solo. She froze, couldn't continue. The maestro had to lead her off the stage."

Brad stared at him, dumbfounded. Leslie! Breaking down in the middle of her solo! After the brilliant way she'd performed in Chicago. "What caused it?" he asked, his eyes darkening in dismay.

Stuart shook his head sadly. "We don't know. All we know is that evidently she was involved with some man, and something went wrong."

Brad frowned. Lorie had said her sister was seeing men now, but he hadn't believed it. "One of the musicians?" he asked.

Stuart sighed. "We don't know. You see, Leslie insists there never was a man."

Brad thought about that. "If it were painful enough she could have blocked it out of her mind," he suggested.

"That's what her doctor thinks."

"This Dr. Berger . . . what does he say about her condition?"

"That she's suffering from a severe emotional depression." Stuart's eyes filled with pain. "If you could see her, Brad."

"I want to," Brad declared.

Stuart shook his head. "She doesn't want anyone to know. We weren't even able to tell her sisters until day before yesterday. And Lorie still doesn't know."

Brad nodded. "Because of that trip to New York."

"At least," Stuart offered philosophically, "she's getting the very best care possible."

Brad ran a hand through his hair. His brows were knit together in frustration. "I wish you could find a way to persuade her to see me."

Stuart remained firm. "I can't let her find out you know. It would upset her too much."

"But isn't there some way . . . ?"

"There's nothing you could do, Brad," Stuart insisted. "It's up to the psychiatrist to reach her."

After Stuart had gone to his own office, Brad sat back down at his desk and reviewed the conversation in his mind. Yes, he mused. If Leslie was really as bad as all that, a psychiatrist was the only person who had a chance of reaching her at this point. But, he reminded himself, that was all the more reason why he should take a trip out to Fairview. After all, *he* was a psychiatrist!

15

He drove out to the sanatorium the next day. I've got to see her, he thought as he drove his car through the gates and up the long driveway leading to the main building. We were so close. I helped her once. Maybe . . . just maybe, I can help her again.

She was sitting at the window seat looking out, the spring sunlight playing across her vacant face as he quietly approached her open door. Dr. Berger, not being appraised of yesterday's conversation with Stuart, had told him to come right up. Stuart had once mentioned Brad to him, had said he was soon to be a member of the family.

His heart leaped as he looked at her. She seemed so small sitting there, so pathetically childlike as she gazed on the rolling lawns and budding flowers outside her window. He took a tentative step farther into the room.

"Les?" he called softly.

She whirled around, stunned by the sound of his voice. When she saw his face, her eyes widened and she seemed almost frightened.

"May I come in, Les?"

The fear left her face. Her shoulders drooped. "Yes."

"It's been a long time, Les." He walked toward her, smiling.

"Why did you come?" she asked in a hollow voice.

"I wanted to, very much." He stopped and eyed

135

her earnestly. "If my being here disturbs you, I'll leave now. Shall I?"

"You shouldn't have come."

"Reverse our positions, Les. If I'd been away and you heard that I was back—and in a hospital—could you stay away?"

She dropped her head, averting her eyes. "It's not the same."

"Tell me why not?" He was being very gentle with her, trying to draw her out without making it appear he was doing so.

"You'll never end up here," she said simply.

He took a step closer to her and raised her face with his hands. "You're not ending up here, Les," he told her with quiet authority. "You're here for help, which you're getting, and you'll leave soon."

"It can happen to anybody," he added firmly. "I'm no exception."

Leslie shook her head. "It could never happen to you."

"Do I really seem that inhuman to you?" When she refused to answer, he went on sadly, "When I learned you were back and I hadn't even been told— well, you'd be sure I was human if you knew how I felt."

She bit her lip and twisted her hands together in her lap. "How?" she asked in a tiny, uncertain voice.

"Unhappy, Les. And very puzzled."

"Why? How could it matter to you?"

"You can ask that?" Brad replied, incredulous.

She gazed at him evenly, almost, he thought in amazement, bitterly. "I can ask it."

"We've been friends for a year. Close friends, I thought." He stopped and studied her, hurt and bewildered.

"Friends aren't responsible for what happens to . . . friends. Are they?"

"Responsible is the wrong word," Brad told her. "If the friendship is real, mutual concern can go very deep."

Leslie remained expressionless. "I see," she said.

"You know how much I wanted you to realize your talent. I even believed I helped you overcome some fears that stood in your way."

Leslie scoffed. "My *talent!*"

"Your rare talent, Les." He regarded her earnestly. "May I talk to you about what happened in Detroit?"

"I don't want to talk about Detroit!" she said, flaring.

Brad nodded. "Then we won't."

"If you try again, I'll ask you to leave."

Brad, astonished by the coldness in her voice, did what he could to placate her. "I'll leave whenever you ask me to," he assured her, adding anxiously, "Not yet, I hope?"

Leslie said nothing, merely turned her back on him and resumed her position at the window. After a moment, however, she turned back and said, almost conversationally, "I hear you're engaged to Lorie."

He nodded. "As of last week."

"Does she"—Her words were halting—"know I'm here?"

"Not yet. She's in New York."

A skeptical look crossed her face. "Why did Lorie go to New York alone if you've just decided to get married?"

"She had some business. She'll be back in a day or so. I'll let her tell you all about it."

Leslie considered that for a moment. "Her New York trip," she mused, "does it have something to do with the book she was writing?"

Brad was surprised. He'd thought Lorie hadn't wanted any of the family to know. "She told you about it?" he asked her.

"You helped her write it," she said.

Brad smiled. "She asked me to read it. I reacted honestly, I hope."

"Did you like it?" Leslie seemed very eager to hear about this.

He shrugged. "That has to be such a personal reaction that I'd rather let you wait for your own. Lorie writes well."

Suddenly Les closed her eyes, and her whole body seemed to shudder. "New York . . . that horrible place," she said tragically, "it will look beautiful to Lorie."

Her mentioning her horror, that was a good sign, Brad thought. He had been told about the New York hospitalization in a subsequent conversation with Stuart yesterday. If she could speak of that, perhaps . . .

"Leslie," he began carefully, "I heard you were hospitalized in New York. I know it was grim—I won't ask you to talk about it. But if we could just go back a little. To Detroit . . ."

"I told you!" she shouted before he could finish, her face suddenly and inexplicably contorted with rage, "I don't want to talk about Detroit!"

"You have to talk about it sometime," Brad said quietly. "That's where it all began."

"Go away!" Leslie cried, really overwrought now. "Go away!"

Brad remained where he was. This anger—it was good. It could trigger the release of all she'd been holding inside her. "Who was the man in your life?" he probed. "The man you were obviously in love with?"

As the question shot through the air, the rage seemed to leave her body and she stood stock-still and looked at him with numb shock written all over her face. Her mouth opened as if she were going to speak, but no words came out. She just stood there, lifeless as a statue.

"Who was the man you loved, Leslie?" Brad persisted. "What did he do to you?"

She was silent for another long moment, and then she spoke as if in a daze. "Who . . . who was the man I was in love with?"

"Tell me, Leslie. It will help me help you."

She stared at him. Her brow was wrinkled. Her eyes were deeply disturbed. "You don't know?" she asked him. "You have no idea?"

Brad shook his head unhappily. "I thought I knew you so well, Leslie," he told her almost reproachfully, "but you never mentioned a man in your life."

"Brad . . ." Suddenly she was composed, almost her old self again. "I know you're trying to help. But . . . I'm very tired. Would you mind leaving me alone now?"

He sighed. Perhaps he should go. In her volatile, unpredictable state, she shouldn't be pressed too far. "All right," he conceded, "I'll go now. If," he added quickly, "you'll let me come again."

Leslie studied him. He felt her eyes probing his face, as if she could see behind it. "All right," she agreed. She managed a small, sad smile. "Good-bye, Brad."

He kissed her gently on the forehead. "Good-bye, Les. See you soon."

Driving back to Genoa City, he tried hard to make some sense out of her words. He could understand her not wanting to talk about Detroit, about the breakdown. But when he'd asked her about the man—the man she'd waited for that night—instead of being angry, she'd seemed almost stunned. It was almost as if she'd expected *him* to know who the man was and why he hadn't shown up.

His mind drifted back over the past year, zeroing in on their various conversations, trying to remember what, if anything, had ever been said about a man in her life. No. He shook his head firmly. She hadn't mentioned anyone. Not a musician, not a young man she'd been in school with, not a single person.

And yet . . . He frowned, careful to keep his eyes on the road. She'd intimated that he *did* know about someone.

Oh, well, he decided as he neared the outskirts of Genoa City. That sort of confusion was not unusual in a case like Leslie's. Probably she thought she *had* told him something.

I'll try again, he told himself determinedly. Maybe if she thinks she told me once, she'll open up again about this mystery man who caused her so much pain and wretchedness. . . .

Leslie remained at the window a long time after he'd gone. It was almost like a dream, she thought, as the sun slowly sank behind the newly blossomed apple trees on the Fairview lawn. Brad Eliot—here, in her room. And, she mused, her brow wrinkling in puzzlement, he had seemed just like the Brad she'd always known. For weeks now, she'd hated him for what he'd done to her in Detroit, had been so sure she'd been wrong about him in the past, that he was not the wonderful person she'd thought, but a cruel, heartless man.

But today he'd been so warm, so gentle with her, so genuinely worried about what was troubling her. If anything, she'd have expected him to be apologetic, embarrassed at the way he'd treated her. But he'd acted as if he didn't have anything to be ashamed of at all, as if he had no idea what she'd meant when she'd told Maestro Fautsch she was expecting the man she loved that night before the concert.

The questions he asked—about Detroit . . . the man I was in love with. He could ask *who* the man was? She shook her head in bewilderment. Could he be that cruel and deceitful? Or . . . is it possible? She took a deep, trembling breath. Is it possible he *didn't know?*

Her reflections were interrupted by the arrival of another visitor—not a disturbing arrival this time, but the welcome appearance of her sister Peggy.

"Oh, look at you!" she exclaimed when she saw her. To her enormous delight, Peg was wearing her cap and gown.

"I wanted to surprise you," her pixielike sister smiled.

"Oh, Peg, you graduated today." She regarded her thoughtfully, an expression of pain creeping across her face. Her youngest sister's graduation, the most important event in her life so far, and she'd missed it!

"I just couldn't feel really *graduated* until my big sister saw me in my cap 'n gown," Peg said brightly.

"Oh, honey." Leslie's voice was choked with emotion. "Oh, Peg, my baby sister. I should've been there."

"Come on, Les," Peg said, not knowing quite how to handle this. "Please . . ."

"I was there when you graduated from grade school," Les said wistfully.

"And you'll be there when I graduate from college? Promise?"

She smiled. "I promise."

Peg fell into her arms, her cap slipping off her head as they embraced. "Les," she said fervently, "I want you home again." Then, worried that she was causing her sister too much anxiety, she amended quickly, "Forget I said it. What's the difference when we can see you out here?" She made an attempt at light chatter. "You've had a lot of visitors, haven't you?"

Les shrugged. "Just the family."

"Well," Peg said, laughing, "that's lots." Then she remembered something Dr. Berger had just told her when she'd asked permission to come up. "I heard Brad was out today."

Leslie said nothing, merely sat looking at her thoughtfully. "He's going to make a super brother-in-law, isn't he?" Peg enthused.

Leslie nodded, almost vacantly. "They must be very happy," she murmured.

Peg rolled her eyes. "Got to be. I know I would be." She sighed enviously. "Lucky Lorie!"

"Peg, I . . ." Leslie began to speak, but broke off, troubled. "I meant to ask Brad while he was here," she managed finally, "but I forgot."

"What?" Peg asked.

"Well, I wondered if he ever got that note I wrote him just before I went to Detroit. The one I asked you to give him."

Peg frowned. "Note?" she repeated, confused.

"You were on your way to school. . . ." Leslie looked down at her hands. Was she crazy? Had there been a note after all? "Doesn't matter," she said abruptly.

"Oh!" Peg exclaimed, remembering. *"That* note! I remember now."

"Then," Leslie breathed, looking at her intently, "he got it."

"Must have," Peg declared. "Sure."

When Les turned away as if she were no longer aware of her presence, Peg took it as a sign she wanted her to leave. "Well," she said lamely, "Mark's waiting. We have to change for the party."

Leslie nodded. "Good-bye, little one," she said, turning back to give her one last hug. "And thanks for letting me share the big event."

"The folks'll be out later," Peg told her. She gave her a bright farewell smile. Then, her eyes widening in sudden remembrance, "Hey—that's right! I gave it to Lorie!"

Leslie stiffened. "Gave what?"

"The note for Brad. I just remembered. When I got downstairs, Lorie came back to the house because she'd forgotten something. When she started back to the office, I asked her to take the note to Brad, and she said she would." She smiled, satisfied. "So I'm sure he got it." She turned toward the door. "Take care, Les. See you soon."

Les forced a smile, unable to speak. Her heart was pounding very fast and her palms were wet with perspiration. Lorie! Peg had given her letter to Lorie!

With a cool deliberation that would have amazed Dr. Berger, she carefully pieced together the pieces of the puzzle that had been hacking away at her since she'd sat down at that piano in Detroit.

She must have read it, she decided with growing agitation. She must have read it . . . and torn it up! *That's* why Brad had never responded to it, why he'd failed to come to the concert without so much as a word of apology. Everything she'd been thinking about him all these weeks was wrong! He *wasn't* heartless and cruel. He was a victim of Lorie's evil maneuvering!

She clenched her hands into tight fists, and her jaw was so tightly set that her teeth bit into each other almost painfully. God help you when I see you, Lorie, her mind cried determinedly. God help you!

16

What a glorious feeling, Lorie thought as the plane that was taking her from New York winged its way back to Genoa City. Indescribable . . . utter euphoria . . . the whole world in my hand. She smiled to herself as she sipped her cocktail. A few months from now I'll board a plane and everyone'll know who I am. Lauralee Brooks, the sensational young novelist!

Closing her eyes, she imagined herself surrounded by eager fans. "Sorry," she would say to them grandly, "I only autograph copies of my books. Happy to oblige—*if* you buy one." My book *will* sell, she thought determinedly, remembering how Dave Larson of Larson-Dunlap, one of the best publishing houses in New York, had said they were all rooting for her when she'd signed the contract that would change her life. I'll do anything—visit every bookstore in the country to sign autographs if that's what it takes. It *will* be a best seller!

Another smile crossed her face as she considered the possibility of a movie sale. Let's see, she mused, who'll play the lead? Robert Redford? Jack Nicholson? Her green eyes gleamed. It was all so fantastic! Everything she'd ever dreamed of!

Leslie, she thought triumphantly, you'll be hearing about *me* now—until you're as fed up as I was of hearing about *you*. Mother once said, if you envy Les, why not compete? So I competed! She took another long sip of her drink. Even Brad was a way of competing with you in the beginning. But the joke's on me! I fell in love! Odd, though, she had to admit, that you bowed out so quickly. One letter, one phone call to him that *I* answered. . . . Odd—but I'm glad. You made it so much easier for me!

When the plane landed, she went directly to the newspaper office. Brad was working on a last-minute interview that had to get in the late edition, and she couldn't wait another minute to see him.

"The conquering heroine returns with no brass band to meet her," she teased when she found him hard at work at his desk. "Not even one fiancé!"

"Didn't you call your parents?" Brad asked, returning her hug warmly.

Lorie shook her head. "Didn't want to see anyone but my man—so I came straight here." Then, unable to contain her excitement, she bubbled, "Oh, Brad, I did it. I *did* it!"

"Contract really all signed and sealed?"

She grinned. "You should've seen the expression on Dave Larson's face when I insisted on my terms!"

Brad smiled at her. "Who knows—he may get a best seller for all his pains."

"May?" Lorie retorted, insulted. *"Will!"* Then her face softened and she kissed him. "Oh, I missed you so damn much, Brad. I was all right during the day, but those nights . . . oh, so lonely!"

"Lorie lonely?" he replied, raising his eyebrows. "Hard to imagine. Hope you got Larson to show you the town at least?"

"No. When I wasn't in his office or on the phone, I walked all over New York—trying to calm down, and missing you."

He took her hand and squeezed it. "Just bear with me a couple minutes more, Lorie, while I finish editing this interview?"

She sighed and moved away, keeping her eyes on him as he tackled the page.

"Know where we're going the minute we leave here?" she asked suddenly, unable to keep still a minute longer.

"Yes," he replied, not looking up.

Her voice became low, husky. "Don't want to stop for dinner—anything. Straight to my apartment, where there aren't any desks or deadlines in our way."

"We'll get there," Brad assured her, "after a short detour."

"Oh, no. No detours."

He looked up then and gave her an apologetic smile. "Lorie, your parents are expecting you. I promised to bring you by."

"You and promises," she muttered, her mouth forming a childlike pout. "That does it." Then she tried again. "But why *tonight?*"

Brad took no notice of her cajoling. "Your parents have something to tell you," he said simply. "We're going—and that's that."

It was a struggle to keep from smiling. It was so wonderful to have a strong, masterful man like Brad— even if she did fight him most of the time.

Naturally, when they arrived at her parents', Stuart and Jennifer were dying to know what she'd been doing in New York.

"Tell us," Jen pleaded. "Don't tease us any longer."

"Well . . . having worked you up to a fever pitch . . ." Lorie smiled impishly. "Mom, Dad, my first novel has been accepted for publication!"

There was a moment of stunned silence, and then she found herself being thoroughly hugged. "Oh, Lorie, dear," her mother said excitedly, "that's wonderful! We're so happy for you!"

"And so proud of you, honey," Stuart added. "Who's publishing?"

"Larson-Dunlap."

Stuart was clearly impressed. "Very good house," he told her.

"Well," Lorie said lightly, trying to seem very

casual and woman-of-the-world about it all, "that's my news. Brad said you had something to tell me."

She was puzzled when Stuart and Jennifer both stiffened and exchanged worried glances. Stuart cleared his throat. "Yes," he said uncomfortably.

Lorie laughed. "Pales into insignificance beside mine, huh?" It was obvious they were feeling foolish about calling her over so urgently.

Then Jennifer spoke up. "It's about Leslie, dear," she said.

"Another city, another ovation?" Lorie groaned inwardly. They'd called her over to talk about *Leslie?*

"It's not good news, Lorie," Stuart told her. "Leslie has been hospitalized."

"What happened?" She stared at them.

"It didn't just happen." Jennifer's face was troubled and unhappy. "She's been hospitalized for a while, but she didn't want her sisters to know until this week."

Lorie looked from one to the other, trying to read their expressions. Why were they backing into it this way? Why didn't they just come out and say what was wrong? "I don't understand," she said, frowning. "You're all being so . . . mysterious."

There was a moment of silence, then Stuart said quietly, "It happened in Detroit, Lorie."

"Detroit?" Lorie felt herself stiffen. "What . . . what happened in Detroit?"

"Midway during her concert, she froze. Couldn't continue. Had to be led from the stage." Stuart stopped. He had become very emotional.

"The maestro said she was expecting a guest who didn't appear," Jennifer continued for him. "He insists it was a man she was in love with. And," she added, "there was a disturbing phone call, apparently." She sighed heavily. "Whatever happened, it was all too much for her."

Stuart broke in then. "She had a complete breakdown, Lorie."

Lorie stood very still. Les. A breakdown. Because

the man she was in love with didn't show up in Detroit . . . and a phone call. . . . "The hospital she's in?"
she asked haltingly.

It was Stuart who answered. "Fairview."

"A . . . a psychiatric hospital." Lorie seemed to
choke on the words. A psychiatric hospital because of
. . . "No," she whispered, more to herself than to anyone around her. "No. Oh, no."

"I'm sorry this had to come on the heels of your
success in New York," Stuart said gently. "But we
had to tell you because Leslie's very anxious to see you.
In fact, she's waiting for you now."

"Leslie wants to see me tonight?" Lorie's heart
began to pound. *Why?* What could it mean?

Stuart nodded. "She's waiting for you."

"But . . . I mean . . ." She began to sputter. This
was crazy! "I don't think I should go tonight. Surely
she needs her rest."

"It's more important for her to see us when she
wants to," Stuart declared.

"It could be a good sign, Lorie," Jennifer put in.
"Wanting to see her family means she's losing some of
that terrible shame she felt when she first came back."

"Yes," Lorie replied, floundering now for something to say that would seem logical. "I can understand
that. Only—" she stopped.

"Only what, Lorie?" Brad, who had said nothing
until now, put a reassuring arm around her shoulders.

She looked up at him. "You knew?" she asked.

He nodded. "I found out by accident."

"I'm just so afraid I might break down in front of
her," she explained to him shakily. "This has been such
a shocker for me."

"You can handle it, Lorie," Brad insisted. "If she
wants to see you, you have to do it."

"Well, yes, naturally." She knew she'd lost. Might
as well face it. "If she wants to see me so much, of
course I'll go tonight." To her mind she sounded very
much the responsible sister doing her duty.

Brad drove her to the sanatorium, but she asked

him to wait for her downstairs, explaining she thought it best to see Les alone. She stopped in the gift shop and picked out an attractive summer sweater, which she had gift-wrapped, and then, following the directions given to her by Dr. Berger, she made her way to her sister's room.

The door was open when she got there, and Les was sitting in a chair, seemingly deep in thought. When she heard the footsteps that stopped in the doorway, she looked up.

Lorie took a deep breath and flashed a cheery smile. "Hi, Les," she said. "How are you, honey?"

Leslie stared at her, and her eyes were like two pieces of steel. "How do you think?" she growled.

"Oh, Les, I'm so sorry." Lorie's face worked itself into an expression of deep concern. "I came as soon as Mom and Dad told me." She walked toward her and attempted to embrace her.

Leslie pulled away with staggering force. "Don't!" she shouted.

"All right, Les. If you don't want to be touched." She held out the package. "Honey, I stopped in the gift shop downstairs and picked this out for you."

When Les made no move to take the present, Lorie began unwrapping it. She held up the sweater. "You can wear it when you go walking in the garden," she said, speaking as one would speak to a senile grandparent. "You'll be well enough to do that soon." She fixed her eyes on her sister earnestly. "You *will* get well soon, honey. You have to. We all love you and want you to be well."

"Do you?" Leslie asked.

"You know I do. I was so unhappy about what happened to you."

Leslie's lip curled in disgust. "You're utterly contemptible," she spat, eyeing her bitterly. "I suppose you're proud of yourself," she went on when Lorie said nothing, merely widened her eyes in stunned surprise. "You did this to me."

"Les, honey . . ."

Leslie didn't let her finish. She had more important things of her own to say. "I have you to thank for being here in this place," she told her bluntly.

Lorie managed—just—to maintain her composure. "You're sick, Les," she said weakly. "I won't hold what you're saying against you."

"I confided in you!" Leslie cried. "Told you I loved Brad. So you moved in, deliberately took him away from me."

"That's not the way it was!"

"Sure!" Les retorted sardonically. "You told me he was helping you with your book. So you could see him behind my back."

"He *was* helping me!" Lorie protested. She was almost frightened by the venom in her sister's voice.

"I was away," Les went on, ignoring her defense. "You moved in on him, played it for all it was worth. You deliberately set out to destroy me. And you did it with your tricks and intrigue."

Lorie's face hardened. She wanted to hurl insults? Well, maybe it was time the *truth* was faced. "You're forgetting one thing," she reminded her coolly. "Brad was never in love with you."

"You never gave me a chance!" Leslie railed at her. "You were too clever for me. You opened the letter I wrote him, and you intercepted my phone call."

"If he had loved you," Lorie replied, "nothing I could have done would have gotten him away from you."

Leslie looked at her as if she were the lowest thing on earth. "Trusting you," she muttered, "that was my mistake."

Lorie met her eyes squarely. "No matter what, Les," she said simply, "Brad does love me."

"He doesn't know what you are," Leslie shot back. "Only I know how contemptible you are."

Lorie shrugged. What did she need this for, anyway? "No matter what you may say," she told her sister flatly, "Brad and I are going to be married." Then, as if to rub in what had happened to her, she added with exaggerated concern, "You can't think straight now, Les, because you're sick. When you're better, you'll see the truth for what it is."

"I know you for the evil liar you are," Leslie retorted. "And someday, somehow, I'll find a way to prove it."

"Don't be so angry, Les." Lorie was almost enjoying this now. "It's not good for you in your condition."

The next thing she knew, the new sweater was flying at her, box and all. "Get out. Get out!" Les screamed wildly. "You conniving tramp!"

She didn't wait to be told again. She hurried out of the room and down the hallway. But as she went to meet Brad, she thought with confidence, what does it matter if she blames me for this? It's only her word against mine. And *she's* in an insane asylum!

Brad was disappointed when he learned that Lorie had gleaned no more in her meeting with Les than any of the others. "She's really in bad shape," Lorie had told him when she'd come down from her room at Fairview that night. "I don't think she knows *what* happened to her anymore."

Brad didn't believe that for a minute. Somewhere inside that tortured head of hers, Leslie knew exactly what had happened in Detroit. She knew who the man she'd tried to phone was, and why she'd broken down on stage and been unable to continue her concert.

She's just blocking it out, he mused as he bent over the galleys at his desk in the office. Whatever it was, it's so painful that she can't bring herself to face it.

Since he'd learned about Leslie's illness, the psychiatrist in him—the man he'd been trained to be but who had been pushed back into a dark corner for over a year now—crept more and more to the fore every day. He was close to Leslie, and he had the training to help her. If anyone could get through to her, he could. And he *would*. Somehow, he'd find the key that would unlock her awful secret. And after that . . . well, then she'd be Leslie again, not that poor creature who spent her days staring listlessly out the window of her hospital room.

He had cleared his desk and was preparing to go out to lunch when Peggy Brooks came bouncing into his office. Peg, the youngest and perhaps peppiest of Stuart's daughters, had just graduated from high school and had taken a job as copy girl with the paper for the summer.

"Hi, Brad!" she chirped when she saw him. "Dad tell you I'm joining the team for the summer?"

He smiled. "He told me. Welcome aboard."

"Thanks. I'm going to love it."

"We'll work your tail off," Brad warned her.

Peg giggled. "Just the right thing for my figure," she countered. "Les always told me that's where half my food showed up."

"I hear you went out to see her on graduation day."

Peg nodded, sobering as she recalled the visit. "In my cap and gown. Dr. Berger told me you'd been out earlier."

"Yes." Brad rose from his desk.

"Brad," Peggy said, stopping him before he could leave the bullpen, "before I forget—Leslie asked me if you ever got her letter. You did, didn't you?"

Brad frowned. "What letter?"

"It was a while back. You know, the one Lorie gave you."

He shook his head. "I don't remember any letter from Les."

"Sure you do," Peg insisted. "It was the day she left for Detroit."

"Peg, will you come in, please?" Stuart was calling his daughter from his office.

"Oh, the boss," Peg said to Brad with an exaggerated grimace. "Got to go."

She rushed off before Brad could question her further. What had she been talking about? He hadn't received a letter from Leslie.

He thought about it as he made his way downstairs and out into the street. Les had written him a letter? The day she'd left for Detroit? Without even realizing where he was headed, he walked straight to the parking lot where he kept his car. It was only after he was seated in the driver's seat and pulling out onto the road that his conscious mind caught up with his unconscious. He was doing what Peg's information demanded he do. He was going out to Fairview to ask Leslie if what she'd said was true.

She didn't seem unhappy to see him, though she didn't exactly rush into his arms when he entered her room. "I came to ask you something," he told her once he'd greeted her and asked the usual things about how she was feeling and whether she'd eaten all her lunch.

"What?" she replied warily.

"You wrote me a letter."

He saw the redness creep over her face and heard the little cry in her voice as she repeated, as if confused, "A letter?"

"You gave it to Peg to bring to me. But she gave it to Lorie to deliver." He faced her curiously. "What was in it, Les?"

Leslie looked down, refusing to meet his eyes. "I don't know what you're talking about," she said in a low, almost unintelligible voice.

"Try to think, Les." He could tell by the way she was acting that she was hiding something.

Suddenly she became almost defiant. "Why is it so important to you?" she demanded.

"Because it's something you did before leaving for Detroit." He took a step toward her. "Maybe I'm grabbing at straws. But I'm trying to find answers—something that will tell me what brought on your breakdown."

Leslie scoffed. "How could a dumb note bring on a breakdown?"

"I don't know, Leslie. I thought perhaps you could help me."

She looked at him for a long moment, and then she said brusquely, "Why don't you go? I'm sure Lorie's waiting for you."

He remained where he was. "Let's forget Lorie for the moment."

"You're going to marry her. You should be with her, not me." She turned away, facing the window. "You can't do anything for me." Then she sighed and muttered, "As far as that letter's concerned, I'm sorry now I ever wrote it."

"Then you do remember writing it?" Brad's eyes were fixed on her intently.

She shrugged. "You say I did."

"Peg said you did."

Slowly she turned around. Her eyes met his, and they were filled with inexplicable pain. "I shouldn't have," she said dully.

He stared at her in surprise. "Why would you say that?"

Quick as a wink, her mood changed and she was angry once again. "Because you're upsetting me with all your questions."

"I'm trying to help you, Leslie."

"You're making me uncomfortable by being here. I wish you'd leave."

He reproved her gently, trying to make her remember that he was a friend. "There was a time when you'd confide in me," he said.

She didn't bite. "I can't confide in anyone," she insisted. "Now please go away and leave me alone."

"The letter, Leslie," he persisted. He would not go until she told him what was in it.

But before he could ask again, she was shouting at him almost hysterically. "It was just a thank-you note for the flowers you sent to me in Chicago!" she cried bitterly. "What else would I have to write you about?" She took a deep, almost choking breath. "Now go!"

He eyed her steadily. There was more to this than she was telling him, much more. A thank-you note wouldn't arouse such anger in her. But he knew he couldn't press her further in this highly inflammatory state. He'd just have to wait until another time. Until she'd calmed down enough to tell him what she'd *really* written.

17

He had the answer, even before she gave it to him. After her initial admission—that she *had* written him a letter—he turned the whole thing over in his mind until he found what had to be the only logical explanation. The note had to have been more than a thank-you note. She wouldn't have been so reluctant to talk about it if it hadn't been.

A call to Lorie revealed nothing. She remembered something about a note, but she didn't know what it said, had simply put it on his desk and forgotten about it. Probably, Brad thought, it had been misplaced, or even thrown out. But the note was the key. Somehow it was connected with that *other* thing she refused to talk about, the man she was waiting for that night in Detroit.

Could it be . . . ? he asked himself as the pieces of the puzzle suddenly fell into place with startling clarity. Yes! It *had* to be! *He* was the man! She had enclosed a ticket to the concert in that thank-you note and she'd been expecting him to be there. And he hadn't phoned, wired . . . anything.

The following evening he returned to Fairview to get the truth. "Leslie," he began with quiet frankness, "you thanked me for the flowers when you called me from Chicago, right after your debut. So there was no need to write a thank-you note. I'm convinced there was more to your letter."

156

She sat there staring at him dully. "No," she said stubbornly.

He leaned toward her. His eyes probed her face. "What else was in that letter?"

She looked away. "Nothing."

"I don't believe you, Leslie." When she refused to respond, he offered his theory, the theory he was certain was correct. "I believe there was a ticket in your letter. A ticket for me for the Detroit concert. When I told you I couldn't go to your Chicago concert, we made a date for me to meet you in Detroit, for your concert there. I didn't see you before you went to Detroit, but I expected to hear from you—expected a ticket for your concert there."

He gazed at her intently. She was listening to him in a totally listless state, her shoulders drooping, her face expressionless. "I thought of going to Detroit," he went on. "I wanted to very much. But when I didn't hear from you, I thought you didn't want me."

She turned toward him then, her eyes filling with pain and bewilderment. "Didn't want you?" she said.

"I thought you were showing me you could stand on your own. So I didn't go because I didn't want you to feel dependent on me.

"But you *did* want me there." he added with certainty. "You *did* want me to hear you play." He took a deep breath. "You did get that ticket for me, didn't you, Les?"

Under such an avalanche of interrogation, Les finally broke. "Yes, yes, yes!" she cried out. Then her whole body drooped again, and tears began to roll down her cheeks.

"Now I can understand why you've been so hostile to me," Brad told her soothingly. "I'm so sorry, Leslie, that I never got your letter. But Lorie put it on my desk and somehow it got misplaced or thrown out. I would give anything if that hadn't happened."

"Would you?" Leslie's voice was low, cynical.

"Yes, Leslie, I would. I'm so sorry I wasn't there

when you expected me, wanted me. You know me well, Leslie. We have a very special friendship. I certainly would have been there with you if I had received your letter."

"Would you have?" She was questioning his every statement as if she couldn't believe he was telling the truth.

"You can believe that, Leslie," he told her, "because it's true." He frowned in frustration. "When you didn't hear from me, why didn't you phone?"

Leslie looked abruptly away. It was almost as if she were blocking him out, had turned her mind off.

"There has to be more to all this," he persisted. "I know you well, Leslie. I know you didn't have a breakdown just because I didn't show up at your concert. There has to be more to all this—much more."

Leslie looked down at her hands. "No more questions," she said in a whispered plea.

Brad studied her. She was clearly distraught. "All right, Leslie," he said resignedly. "I'm not going to press you any further tonight. But one way or the other, I'm going to find out the rest of the story you're hiding. I'm convinced there's more—*much* more—to it." He rose and offered a warm smile. "Good night, Leslie. I'll see you tomorrow."

Driving home, he puzzled over it. He wasn't surprised to learn that she had sent him a ticket after all; his surprise had been in thinking she *hadn't* sent it. And the fact that it had been misplaced . . . well, his desk was so cluttered with papers that it was hard to make sense out of anything on it. But if she had wanted him, and he hadn't shown up . . . wouldn't the most logical thing for her to have done have been to phone? They had been on the friendliest of terms. Surely she knew he wouldn't mind her calling him.

Suddenly a light exploded in his mind. Of course! There *had* been a phone call! Maestro Fautsch had told the Brookses that Les had said it was a phone call that had upset her. How could he have forgotten that?

But, he remembered, his elation ebbing, the phone call hadn't been to him. He thought back to the night of her concert. That was the night . . . yes, the night Lorie had moved into her new apartment. He had helped her lift some boxes and hang a picture or something. But they hadn't been at her apartment the entire evening. No, he distinctly remembered taking her back to his room to pick up her manuscript and typewriter she'd left there. And there hadn't been a phone call.

But . . . wait. His mind grasped for total recall. He hadn't stayed in his room the whole time. He'd gone down to the restaurant to talk to Sally for a few minutes, and Lorie had remained there alone. Could Leslie have phoned him then? Could she have talked to Lorie before she went on stage?

He didn't understand any of it. Lorie had mentioned no call and even if there *had* been one, he couldn't imagine why it would upset Les to the point of desperation. No. He must be on the wrong track. But just to make sure, he decided to question Lorie.

"I'm convinced she phoned someone in Genoa City," he told her when he'd arrived at her apartment for the quiet evening they'd planned to spend together. "And since she was waiting for me, I'd be the obvious one she'd want to talk to. But I received no call." He regarded her intensely. "You were with me that night, Lorie."

Lorie pursed her lips in deliberation. "Was I?" she mused.

"You came up to my room. We were talking about Leslie opening in Detroit that night."

"Oh, yes." Lorie nodded abstractly. "I do remember now."

"I remember wondering why she hadn't sent me a ticket for her concert. Then I left the room to go talk to Sally."

Lorie looked at him blankly. "That I don't remember."

He tried to prod her. This was important. "I left

you in the room alone for quite a while. You were working on your book. The typewriter was in my room. Do you remember now?"

"Hmmm," she mused. "Yes, I think so."

"While you were there alone"—Brad was very anxious now—"did Leslie phone me? Did you talk to her?"

Lorie widened her eyes. "Brad," she replied petulantly, "why would you think that?"

"Process of elimination. I'm positive Leslie made that call to someone in Genoa City."

Lorie smiled skeptically. "You're theorizing, Brad."

"Lorie, it's the only thing that makes sense. I'd be the logical one for her to phone since she was waiting for me. But I didn't get any call. Certainly your parents didn't, or they'd have said something. And Chris and Peggy would have no reason to hide it if Leslie had called them."

Suddenly Lorie was full of indignation. "And you think *I* have a reason to hide it?" she snapped.

He considered that. There was so much here, beneath the surface. Lorie was in love with him. Maestro Fautsch had said Leslie was in love with the man she was waiting for in Detroit. And *he,* as he now knew for sure, was that man! If there had been a phone conversation between two women, both of them in love with him . . .

"You told me you and Les were very close. That she confided everything to you," he said, beginning a new tack in order to get to the bottom of this.

"That's right," Lorie replied evenly.

Brad regarded her. "If Leslie were in love with me, she would have told you, wouldn't she?"

Lorie pondered that. "I think so," she said slowly. "I can't be sure, of course, Les being so introverted."

Brad persisted undaunted, sure he was on to something now. "I think it's possible she did tell you she loved me, and your sense of rivalry with her made you say something to discourage her."

"That's not true!" Lorie retorted, her eyes flashing fire. "And I resent your saying it!"

"You could have taken the call to me, Lorie. Told her you and I were having an affair. Then, when you learned how Les reacted, how that call threw her into an emotional breakdown, you were afraid to say anything about it for fear you'd be blamed." His eyes bored into her face. "Is that the way it happened, Lorie?"

"No! It isn't!" she shouted. "You're making me out a monster!"

"No," he said, shaking his head sadly, "just a frightened, confused girl who's afraid to admit what she did to her sister."

"Brad, I swear it!" Lorie cried passionately. "I never took a call from Leslie." A tear glistened on her dark lashes. "I love Les. I want her to get well."

He wanted to believe her. Oh, how he wanted to believe her! But the more he thought about it, the more his theory seemed to make sense. Lorie, still consumed by the jealousy that had eaten away at her since childhood, had learned of Leslie's feelings for him and decided to use everything in her power to keep the relationship between the two of them from blossoming into anything more than it already was. That would explain why Leslie hadn't wanted her sisters to be told of her breakdown at first, and why, when Stuart had finally convinced her they should be told, she'd asked to see Lorie immediately. Undoubtedly, he surmised, becoming more and more excited, a confrontation had taken place the night he'd driven Lorie out to Fairview. Lorie had emerged from Les' room a little flustered, as he recalled, but she'd said little about the visit other than Les was in a bad state.

A bad state! No doubt! And with damned good reason, if all he suspected was correct.

But before he could do anything regarding Lorie, he had to be sure. Again he went to Fairview; again he plied Les with questions concerning that all-important night.

"Leslie," he demanded sternly, "I want the truth. The person you talked to from Detroit the night of your breakdown . . . was it Lorie?"

Leslie looked at him calmly. "Suppose you ask Lorie that question, Brad," she said simply.

That pride of hers! That damned sense of fair play! How like her to refuse to point a finger at anyone.

"I did ask Lorie," he told her. "She said she didn't talk to you."

Leslie's eyes darkened, but she remained composed. "Then why are you asking me?" she asked him. "She's the woman you're in love with, the one you're going to marry."

He eyed her carefully. "But I *am* asking you, Les."

She shrugged. "What makes you think Lorie's the one I talked to that night?"

"I've given it a lot of thought—from all angles. You sent me a ticket to your Detroit concert and I didn't show up."

"Because you never received my letter."

"When I didn't arrive, the most natural thing in the world would have been for you to call me, find out if I were on my way."

Her expression remained enigmatic. "You think so?" she parried.

"I'm sure of it. And I'm sure now you *did* call. But I was out of my room, talking with Sally. Lorie was waiting there for me, working on her book." His eyes were fixed on her face. "I think you made the call and she took it."

Les looked straight at him. "You said you asked her and she denied it."

He sighed and shook his head. "I'm afraid I can't believe her, Les. I think her sense of rivalry made her tell you something to discourage your feelings about me."

When Leslie refused to respond one way or the other, merely continued to sit passively, looking at him, her blue eyes expressionless, he said appealingly, "I have to find out the truth, Leslie."

"For my sake?" she asked him without feeling. "Or your own?"

He rose from his chair and took a step toward her. "For both of us," he said simply. Then he nodded his head as if satisfied. "I know now I've found the answer."

Leslie smiled enigmatically. "It's all theory, Brad."

But he wouldn't be put off any longer. "It was Lori who took your call, wasn't it?" he demanded. And when she remained silent, he said with real conviction, "Your refusal to answer is my answer, Leslie. It was Lorie who did this to you."

That night he broke his engagement to Lauralee Brooks.

Dr. Berger was ecstatic about Leslie's improvement. It was almost, he told Brad when he stopped by his office to discuss her case, as if a deft surgeon had gone into her brain and removed a splinter that was pricking her conscious mind, paralyzing it with pain. "I know it's you who has been responsible for this," he said gratefully. "The family told me you were a friend of Leslie's. I didn't realize how good a friend until you started coming to see her."

There was one thing, however, that Brad needed to know before he would consider the splinter removed and Leslie on her way to total recovery.

"May I come in, Les?" he asked her when, after his meeting with Dr. Berger, he made his way to her room. "I have so much to say to you."

Les smiled, really smiled happily at him for the first time since she'd been at Fairview. "Be my guest," she replied lightly. "What do you have to tell me?"

He looked at her, his dark eyes deep with feeling. "So much," he said softly. "Now that I know everything."

Leslie looked at him quizically. "Do you know everything—now?"

"Everything, Leslie. Except . . ." He took her hand. "What did you say in your letter besides asking me to come to Detroit for your concert?"

Leslie sat very still for a long moment. Then, "I told you what was in my heart, Brad."

His eyes searched her face. "What was it?"

She sighed and withdrew her hand. "It seems so long ago," she said vaguely.

Brad wouldn't accept that answer. "You told me you were in love with me, didn't you?"

"Yes." She was unable now to meet his eyes.

Brad gaped at her. "I never knew, never had any idea."

Leslie gave a small smile. "I know."

"If I had known . . ." he began, but he couldn't think how to phrase himself, and Leslie broke in before he could begin again.

"I know you were never in love with me. I can accept that now."

Brad took her chin in his hand and very gently tilted her face so that their eyes met. "You're very special to me, Leslie."

She nodded. "You've proved that in so many ways."

"I'll always be here for you. Always know you can depend on me."

She loosened his hand from her face and her eyes clouded. "Even when you marry Lorie?"

He answered very quietly. "There won't be a marriage, Les."

She looked at him in surprise. "You can't forgive her?"

"It isn't a question of forgiveness."

"Then what?"

He frowned, becoming introspective. "In bringing everything out into the open," he said slowly, "I learned something about myself, too."

"What?"

"That I never really loved Lorie." He saw her expression of shock, was aware of the way she suddenly caught her breath. "It was an enormous physical attraction," he went on. "Nothing more."

Leslie's voice quavered. "And her feelings for you?"

"A combination of things, but not love. It was physical attraction, proximity, and the rivalry she felt with you."

Leslie nodded ironically. "She wanted you because she knew I did."

"Don't be too hard on your sister," Brad begged her, knowing the bitterness she must be feeling. "She's a very complex young woman. While you and your parents can't see it or understand it, what caused that old rivalry is very real to Lorie."

"She was the girl who had everything," Leslie argued.

"But," Brad reminded her, "from the time she was a small child she believed she was second best in the eyes of your parents."

Leslie gasped. "They loved her as much as they loved me."

"But *your* needs took their time and attention. Lorie grew up jealous of that. She's carried those feelings with her into her adult life."

Leslie thought about that, realized it was true, and sighed. "Poor Lorie. Suffering from a jealousy that had no basis in fact." Then she looked at him with interest. "You seem to understand her so completely."

"Finally," he agreed, "I think I do. Now that everything is out in the open."

"No more secrets," Leslie said.

"Total-truth time."

She smiled. "It's a beautiful relief."

"Now it shouldn't be too long before you're completely well. Then we can help you build a new future for yourself."

Leslie seemed almost incredulous. "I didn't believe I'd ever think of a future again."

"You can look forward now, Les," he assured her gently. "The past can be forgotten."

"You seem so confident."

He nodded firmly. "And I'm going to make you confident in yourself," he told her. "I don't say it will all come at once, but one day the girl with the golden talent will challenge the world again. And win." He put his arm around her, and like a lost child who has just found its way home, she laid her head on his strong, protective chest.

"Trust me, Leslie," he said huskily, enfolding her in a warm, all-encompassing embrace. "Believe in your future as I believe in you."

18

It's such a beautiful, beautiful world, Leslie thought wonderingly as she gazed out her bedroom window onto the oak trees that ringed the lawn and dropped orange and red leaves onto the soft grass. *Her* bedroom. In the Brooks house—not that lonely room at Fairview, or that horrible, ugly place in New York that had bars on the windows. But, no. She wouldn't think about New York. Or even Fairview. All that was behind her now. Way, way behind her.

She'd been home since the beginning of the summer and now it was fall and *so much* had happened! For one thing, she was playing the piano again. All those months she'd been hospitalized she was sure she'd never touch a piano again. But now she was not only playing —she had actually given another concert with the Mid-America Symphony. Maestro Fautsch had come to see her before she'd even been released from Fairview, and told her he was expecting her to perform in St. Louis as scheduled. And although she'd been terrified at the very idea of it, Brad had soothed her fears and encouraged her and she'd walked out on that stage and given her best performance yet.

Brad. Her mouth turned up in a dreamy smile at the thought of him. She had him to thank for everything. As always. They'd become very close in the last few months—man-woman close, not like the guru-and-worshipful-follower relationship they'd had before her breakdown. They'd been together constantly, drinking in the wonder of having found—really found—each other, thrilling to every touch of hands, every stirring, powerful kiss.

Brad had gone to St. Louis with her, and when they got home, when she was feeling relaxed and snug and more secure than she'd ever felt in her life, he had done the thing she'd dreamed of his doing for almost two whole years. He had asked her to marry him.

She closed her eyes as that incredible memory washed over her. They'd been at the house telling her parents about her triumph, and when Stuart and Jen had left them alone, they'd sat on the piano bench together and Les had impulsively played a pop song, laughing at the incongruity of a concert artist indulging in something so mundane.

"Can this be the same girl I used to visit at Fairview—how many weeks ago?" Brad asked her teasingly. "The girl who was so withdrawn she could barely communicate?"

Leslie had stopped playing and turned to him with a smile. "The same girl. It's hard for me to believe, too."

He took her hand. "It's a beautiful thing to see, Les."

Rapturously, she had moved closer to him. "I owe it all to you," she told him sincerely. "Everything." She shook her head. "I wonder what would have happened to me, what I would have done, without you." And then she had smiled. "A man from out of nowhere. Who by chance came to Genoa City."

"If it hadn't been for your father's blind faith—his offering a total stranger a job—we never would have met." His eyes grew deep with feeling. "Now," he said softly, "I'm asking *you* to take me on blind faith."

"Hardly blind faith," Leslie had scoffed, not realizing what he was leading up to.

He had tightened his grip on her hand. "You don't understand what I'm trying to say."

She had frowned. This abrupt switch from teasing

to seriousness . . . it was unlike him. "What," she whispered, "are you trying to say?"

And then he had come out with it, his voice low and heavy with emotion. "I'm asking you to marry me, Les."

She had been stunned, utterly dumbfounded. She had hoped, of course. Often wished . . . But she hadn't really thought it could ever happen. It was almost like a dream, yet her eyes were wide open and Brad Eliot's face was close enough to kiss. Oh, how she loved him! He was the world to her—the sun, the moon, the stars . . . everything.

"I've . . . I've waited so long for you to say that," she had said, her voice a choked whisper, her eyes filling with tears of pure joy. "I hoped you would, but never believed it would actually come true." She had taken his hand and raised it to her damp cheek. "I love you so much—more than anything in my life. And," she had added fervently, "I want you. Oh, God, how I want you."

Brad's eyes had darkened with passion. "As I want you."

And then Leslie had done the hardest thing she had ever done in her life. "I have to find myself as a person before I'll be ready to be a wife," she had told him, mustering all her inner strength to keep from making what she knew would be a mistake at this point. "When I come to you, I want to be worthy of you in every way. A whole person."

He had shaken his head. "I want you now, Les." It was a command, not a wish.

"First let me do this thing for myself," she had pleaded, her face blazing with earnestness. "Let me grow up, be secure as a woman within myself. There are still a lot of knots that have to be untied inside of me before I'm ready to share my life with the man I love."

He hadn't wanted to accept that answer, had urged her to change her mind and come to him as she was, to let him help her with the things that still needed to be done. But she had remained firm. She wanted to be his wife more than anything on earth, but it had to be right. And it couldn't be—yet.

For one thing, she had to get used to the idea of being married, of being loved totally and utterly by this big, bronzed hulk of a man. She, who had never expected any man to love her, needed time to take it all in, absorb it, live with it, really come to accept it.

And then there were things about Brad that had to be worked out. He had opened up somewhat about his past before he had asked her to marry him. He had told her he was from Chicago, that he had been a doctor there—a psychiatrist and neurosurgeon—and that he was thought dead because a man who had stolen his car had died in a crash. The part about his being a psychiatrist hadn't been too surprising, really. She'd known he had to know a great deal about people's heads from the way he had helped her all those long months, both before and after her breakdown. But he had also told her something disturbing—that there had been a woman in his life in Chicago, a woman named Barbara Anderson, whom he had loved very deeply at one time. And that was one of the things she felt they needed to work out between them. She needed to know just where the relationship with Barbara had stood before he left Chicago, and whether there was any chance—any chance at all—that he wasn't completely over it.

The time has come for us to get all this straightened out, she thought now as she turned from the window to prepare for her date with this still somewhat mysterious man of hers. It's been months since he proposed. I told him then that I wanted there to be total honesty between us, and he asked me to give him a little more time, just as I asked him for more time to get my head together. Well, time is passing, and I'm growing stronger and more confident every day. Surely he is ready to give me at least a *few* of the answers.

"Brad," she asked earnestly when he called for her not long afterward. "Can we go someplace and talk?"

He knew, as he always knew everything about her, that she had something important to discuss with him. And he never passed up the chance to let her get things off her chest.

"Yes, Les," he agreed. "If that's what you want."

He took her to his room, that very room where he'd spent so much time with Lorie, but Lorie's ghost was vanquished now and there was no one there but Brad and Les, two people who loved and trusted each other, and had no fear of ghosts, past, present, or future.

Or, at least, so Leslie hoped would be the case tonight.

"Brad," she told him seriously, accepting the glass of wine he poured for her and straining toward him as she sat in his old, worn easy chair, "I want you to tell me about yourself. I want to know everything."

He looked at her for a long moment, and then he nodded, almost as if he'd been expecting it. "Before I do," he said slowly, beseechingly, "there's one thing I beg of you."

Her eyes were fixed on his face. "What?" she replied.

He took her hand. "Believe in me."

"I want to, Brad," she told him softly. "More than anything else in the world."

And then he began his story, going back to the beginning, most of which she already knew. He'd been born in Quincy, the son of Dr. James Eliot, a general practitioner. His father had wanted Brad to follow in his footsteps—had dreamed of it all his life—but Brad had been turned off by the long hours and lack of money in a general practitioner's life, and he had turned instead to the more lucrative fields of neurosurgery and psychiatry.

"Maybe you have to know my father, Les, to understand how I hurt him," he said, his eyes growing reflective and unable to hide the pain he felt. "Every fiber of his being was dedicated to helping people. If he never got paid—and there were lots of times when he didn't—he couldn't have cared less."

But Brad wanted more, much more. Breaking from the family and causing great bitterness as a result, he had gone to Chicago after finishing his internship and had gone into practice at the largest, most impressive hospital in the city.

It was there that he'd met Barbara Anderson, the pretty, blond nurse who sometimes moonlighted as a model.

"We lived together for about a year," he confessed to Les, the words causing her to stiffen defensively, though he had told her before that it was all behind him now. "She wanted to get married, but I wasn't ready for that kind of thing.

"Then she got pregnant,"

Leslie's hands grasped the arm of her chair. She felt the room spinning around her.

"I told her to get an abortion," Brad went on, bravely plowing through the story, knowing the pain he was handing this beautiful, lovely young woman who loved him so desperately, but unable to stop now that the moment of truth had come. "I certainly didn't want the responsibility of a child. As far as I was concerned, the matter was settled."

"And," Leslie asked in a small, stunned voice, "she had an abortion?"

Brad took a long drink of his wine. "She said she would. Then she moved away. I didn't see her again for three years, when she moved back to Chicago and we began dating again."

He rose from the bed on which he'd been sitting and began to pace the small room, his long, nervous strides making it necessary to make quick, sharp turns in quick succession. "I was called into the hospital one day," he went on, lost now in these memories he'd so long repressed. "An emergency. A child had taken a bad fall . . . needed immediate surgery." He stopped and ran a hand across his heavily perspiring brow. "I was just beginning to operate when I heard a nurse say, 'Barbara Anderson's child.' "

"*Your* child?" Leslie gasped, almost uncomprehendingly.

Brad nodded. His face was agonized. "I was stunned," he said in a low, incredulous voice. "Barbara had a child she'd never told me about. And then it hit me. My God! He must be my child, too!" He began to pace again. "Barbara had never had the abortion. This was my son, a son I never knew I had. And now it was up to me to save his life."

He looked at her, and his eyes were those of a man with a terrible, unspeakable secret. "I . . . I performed the operation, did the best I could. But it wasn't enough. When I left the operating room, my son was dead."

Devastated, her heart crying out to him, Leslie rushed to him, put her arms around him, and without saying a word, held him close.

"Can you understand why I didn't want to tell you?" he cried wretchedly. "Why I thought it best not to confide in you?"

"Yes," Leslie whispered, "I can understand."

"I . . . I don't know how you'll feel about . . . everything . . . now. But at least there aren't any more secrets, Les. You know the whole story."

Leslie held him for a long moment, then she gently released her arms and turned away, stunned and disturbed.

He took an anxious step toward her. "Surely you can understand the torment I felt," he said, obviously fearing she wouldn't be able to forgive him for not telling her he had had a child until now. "What I went through—discovering I had a son, then seeing him die —all within the span of a few minutes."

"So much torment that you ran away," she said quietly.

He swallowed hard. "I had to put my life back together, get some perspective. My whole world had been torn apart, Les."

"What about your parents' world?" she couldn't

keep from crying. "To let them think you were dead—
it seems so . . . insensitive . . . so cruel. . . ."

"It *was* insensitive, Les," he admitted. His jaw
was set grimly. "I can't deny that. I can only say that
at the time I was caught up in my own problems."

"Did you think you could solve them by running
away?"

He shook his head. "The only thing I knew was I
had to get away."

Leslie was silent while she pondered that. Then
she asked him the frankest question yet. "How do I
know," she queried bluntly, "you wouldn't do that
again if there were a big enough problem?"

He gave a little cry. "That's not fair, Les. It's because of what happened before that I'm the man I am
now."

"And you expect me to believe you've actually
faced the past, come to grips with your problems? That
you're not still running away?"

He looked at her squarely, and his eyes were plead-
ing—and overflowing with love. "I've found a life
that's brought me contentment. I have no desire to
change it—in any way."

Leslie stared at him. For a moment he thought she
was going to turn and leave. But she had no intention of
doing that. There was so much more to be settled. "I'm
sorry, Brad," she told him, "but I think there have to be
some changes."

He blanched. "What are you saying, Les?"

"You have two parents who think you're dead,"
she said with quiet authority. "You're going to see them,
let them know you're alive."

The Eliot house in Quincy was a modest old frame
affair on a pleasant, tree-lined street. As Leslie stepped
out of the car and walked up the sidewalk, she noticed
a rose bush—sleeping, of course, now that it was almost
winter—climbing up one side of the house, and cheerful yellow curtains hanging at the windows.

It's a lovely, comfortable-looking place, she

thought as she reached the porch and pressed the doorbell. The kind of place nice people would live in. Her stomach lurched as she heard the bell ringing inside. I hope, she prayed, we're doing the right thing. At least my coming first to break the news will buffer some of the shock.

She stood very straight as the door opened and a pleasant-looking woman with a warm, lined face and gray-streaked hair that was cut short and attractively waved faced her curiously.

"Are you Mrs. Eliot?" she asked.

"Yes," the woman answered, "I am."

Leslie smiled at her. "My name is Leslie Brooks. I'm a friend of your son's."

A shadow crossed the woman's face. "My dear," she said sadly, "my son's dead."

"Please, Mrs. Eliot," Leslie urged, "may I come in? I have a lot of explaining to do."

The woman studied her for a moment and then, obviously deciding she was someone deserving of at least a little hospitality, stepped aside and ushered her in.

"Is Dr. Eliot at home?" Leslie asked, looking around the gracious, comfortable living room.

"No, he's out on house calls." Mrs. Eliot faced her with interest. "You said you had some explaining to do, Miss Brooks."

Leslie nodded. "As I told you, I'm a friend of your son's. A very close friend."

"You mean," the older woman corrected, "you *were* a friend."

Leslie met her eyes. "No. I *am* a friend." As Mrs. Eliot stiffened and opened her mouth in surprise, Leslie went on quickly. "Brad wasn't killed in that automobile accident, Mrs. Eliot. The body that was identified as his was that of a thief who robbed him, knocked him out, and stole his car."

Brad's mother stepped back and took hold of a chair for support. "You're saying that . . . ?" Her eyes were wide, disbelieving.

Leslie spoke gently. "Brad is alive, Mrs. Eliot. Very much alive and well."

"But . . ." The woman was practically beyond speech. "If he didn't die . . . if he's alive . . ."

Les knew she was wondering why he'd let them go on thinking he was dead, and feeling that that was something Brad should explain himself, she offered only a superficial explanation. "When he learned the thief had been identified as him, it was too late to spare you. You had already been notified he was dead."

Mrs. Eliot shook her head and tears sprang to her dark eyes. "I can't believe it. My son . . . alive."

"He's anxious to become reconciled with you and his father," Leslie told her. "He's outside in the car . . . waiting."

Leslie cried openly along with Mrs. Eliot as Brad walked slowly into the house and enfolded his mother in a long, highly emotional embrace. The scene was repeated later when Dr. Eliot came home, and in the course of the evening all the questions were answered, all the old bitterness and resentments set to rest. The Eliot family was reunited in love and forgiveness.

"We have a great deal to thank you for, Leslie," Dr. Eliot said as the night drew to an end at last and, however reluctantly, she and Brad prepared to drive back to the airport. Brad had told them it had been her idea to come here.

"You brought our son home to us," Mrs. Eliot added warmly.

Brad put his arm around Leslie and held her very close. "She's going to be a part of our family," he told them. "Whenever the lady's ready, she's going to be my wife."

Leslie smiled up at him. And in her eyes was a message. There was no need to wait any longer.

19

Lorie Brooks dabbed a generous amount of her exotic perfume behind her ears and surveyed herself in the bedroom mirror. Not bad, she thought as she studied the long, dark-green satin gown that set off her eyes and showed to advantage her firm young body. A little high necked for the author of the hottest book of the season, maybe, but just right for Les' wedding.

Les' wedding. She could think of it now with very little emotion. Naturally, she'd been devastated when Brad had broken *their* engagement, but in a way she hadn't really been surprised. All her life, she'd realized with bitter resignation, people had turned from her to Leslie. Why shouldn't Brad do the same?

She also knew that, no matter how she'd tried to deny it, she'd treated Les badly. She never should have read that letter and kept Brad from seeing it. And, knowing how sensitive her sister was, she shouldn't have been so blatant about her affair with Brad when she'd called from Detroit that night. But . . . She sighed. She'd wanted him so much. . . .

Oh, well, she thought, turning from the mirror and reaching for the soft mink cape she'd bought with part of her advance on the book royalties, that was a long time ago. It's past now, and Les is happy, has everything she wants. And I . . . She smiled a little smile of satisfaction. I have everything I want, too. The book will be out soon, and it's going to be the greatest seller of all time. Lauralee Brooks is going to become a household word. And men . . . well, I'll probably be *glad* I didn't tie myself down to a small-town guy like Brad. I'll have men of the world chasing after me. Shipping magnates . . . movie producers . . . movie *stars!*

She swung out of the apartment and headed for her snappy red sports car, another recent gift to herself. Better hurry on over to the house if she didn't want to be late for the ceremony.

As she drove through the streets of Genoa City, her heart constricted a little. What would they all say when they saw her there? She'd told the family she wouldn't be attending the wedding. Not because she couldn't bear to see Les and Brad married—she'd made that abundantly clear—but because she thought it might be . . . well, awkward, in view of the fact that she and Brad had been lovers. Leslie, however, ever the peacemaker, had told her it was up to her, that she was willing to forget the past and that she would be welcome if she changed her mind. Still . . . Lorie prepared herself for the worst as she maneuvered the car into the closest parking place she could find to the house.

Some twenty people—all close friends of the Brookses'—were gathered in the living room as she slipped in and made her way quietly up the stairs. She found the family in the master bedroom, putting the finishing touches on Les' gown. Everyone looked around as she entered. The two sisters' eyes met in the mirror as Lorie stopped uncertainly.

"If you'd rather I leave, Les," she said softly, "tell me."

While everyone else remained rooted to the spot, Leslie turned to face her. "No, Lorie," she said sincerely. "By all means stay."

Lorie nodded and offered a small smile. "I'll be downstairs." She turned to go. "And Les?" Suddenly she turned back.

"Yes?"

"Good luck."

A few minutes later, left alone at her own insistence, Leslie stood in her long white gown, with its wide, heavily jeweled collar and lush, white mink cuffs, and bowed her head in a silent prayer of thanksgiving. This was her wedding day. The day she felt she'd been waiting for practically all her life. In just a few more minutes she would become the wife of Dr. Bradley Eliot.

Her heart fluttered a little at the thought of it. She, simple, unbeautiful, totally unsophisticated Leslie Brooks, was going to be joined forever to the most wonderful, brilliant, handsome, exciting man in the world! Every time she thought about it, it seemed like a dream. To think that after all she'd been through—the shy, unattractive, insecure years, the blossoming out only to find that the man she loved seemed to be in love with her sister, the terrifying mental collapse in Detroit, the horror of New York, and the despair of Fairview— she had found the greatest happiness a woman can hope for: a perfect, totally fulfilled love.

Slowly, lovingly, she began to twist the diamond and pearl engagement ring that sparkled on her finger, and then she remembered she shouldn't be wearing it. She must remove it now—and make room for her wedding band. She smiled as she placed it in her jewelry box and thought back to the moment when she'd told Brad she was ready to plan the wedding. How happy he'd been! How wonderfully his eyes had shone, how tenderly he had looked at her! She had told him after that evening with his parents in Quincy, when Brad Eliot had officially become a man with a past again. And he'd gone for the ring himself, wanting to surprise her with its design.

"Oh, Brad," she'd said eagerly when he'd slipped it on her finger, "it's all been such an adventure."

"I promise you," he had said, smiling, "that our whole life is going to be an adventure."

There had been a few small problems to work out, a few loose ends that had had to be tied up. Brad, now that his secret about his child was out, had confessed to her that he had been haunted by the thought that perhaps the child needn't have died on the operating table—that perhaps another, more skilled surgeon would have been able to save him. And Leslie, filled with unexpected new courage, had taken the bull by the horns and gone to Chicago, the place where it had all begun, and had spoken to the anesthesiologist who had been in the operating room with Brad that day. And he had told her in no uncertain terms that Dr. Bradley Eliot had done everything humanly possible to save the child, that the boy's injuries had been so massive that he had had no chance of recovery, no chance at all. And then she had gone back to Genoa City and told Brad. And he had been a new man.

For a while she had even thought he might decide to go back into medicine now that his guilt was cleared away, and she had told him she would be willing to accept any decision he made regarding his future. But he hadn't wanted to go back. Ever. To her joy, he wanted to stay right here in Genoa City, continue working on the *Chronicle,* live with her and love her in the town she'd lived in all her life.

And so it was settled. All their problems were behind them—the future loomed ahead, bright and beautiful.

Leslie started as a knock sounded at the door and her father's voice called out to her.

"Ready, honey?"

She opened the door and fell into his arms as he greeted her for the last time as a daughter of the house.

"How can I begin to thank you?" she whispered, her eyes filling with tears. "You've taught us so well. And now . . . it's time to leave." She looked up at him and saw his handsome face through a watery blur. "I'll miss you."

"I'll miss you, darling," he told her. "You can't know how much."

Leslie smiled and dabbed at her face with a tissue. "Until a short time ago, you were the man in my life. For so many years. I . . . I never thought I'd meet a man who could ever compare. Until I met Brad." She kissed him lightly on the cheek. "Thank you for so much, Dad. Your patience. Your understanding. Your love."

Stuart looked at her for a long moment, and when he spoke, his voice was hoarse. "It's not easy, when a man has daughters, to see them grow up and go off to other men. I don't have to tell you, Les, you've always been very special." He took her hand and squeezed it. "Be happy, honey. Be happy."

Then he tucked her hand in the crook of his arm and gently led her toward the top of the stairs.

Brad stood next to Greg Foster before the flower-banked fireplace in the Brooks living room. Les had asked Chris to be her matron of honor, and Brad, following her lead, had asked Snapper to stand up for him. But Chris' husband unfortunately had had to go to Denver for a symposium this week, so Brad had asked Snapper's brother Greg to take his place, a request Greg had graciously accepted.

He glanced at his watch. Seven o'clock on the dot. In just a few seconds Leslie would come down those stairs to take her place beside him. Forever.

His heart was filled with happiness. He loved her so much, had so much to thank her for. For all that he had helped her in the past, he was sure he would never be able to repay her. Single-handedly, she had turned him from a tortured man with no past and riddled with doubts about the future, into a happy, forward-looking human being. She had led him back, back to his family, back to his past, and in doing so had wiped out all the agony. He was whole now, and there was nothing he wouldn't do for her. He had even, at her insistence, gone to see Barbara Anderson, had told her about the ghastly mix-up that led to her identifying a dead body as his. And although he had known from the look on her face that she still loved him, he had explained about Leslie and told her she must look to a new future, just as he was doing.

And now that future was about to begin. He stood very straight as the pianist struck up the strains of the "Wedding March." With love-filled eyes, he turned to look at the staircase, where first Chris, and then Les, arm in arm with her father, were slowly, majestically, descending.

His heart jumped as he saw how beautiful she was in her long, perfectly fitted wedding gown and the billowing fingertip veil that could not hide the rapturous look on her face. Oh, Leslie, he thought, his whole body flooding with warmth, you are everything I want in life.

He took his place next to her as her father led her to the small altar that had been erected in front of the fireplace. Reverend Martin, the Brooks family pastor, stood before them looking very solemn, but clearly very pleased to be performing this ceremony.

"Dear friends," he said in a full, rich voice, "we are gathered here in the presence of God to unite this man and this woman in holy marriage, which is instituted of God, regulated by His commandments, blessed by our Lord Jesus Christ, and to be held in honor among all men. Let us therefore reverently remember that God has established and sanctified marriage for the welfare, happiness, and preservation of mankind.

"Let us pray."

The wedding party and their guests bowed their heads as he asked the Lord's blessing on this union.

"Almighty and ever-blessed God, whose presence is the happiness of every condition, and whose favor hallows every relation, we beseech Thee to be present during this wedding ceremony and be favorable to Thy servants in their acts and covenants."

The prayer ended, Brad turned to Les. "Rise up, my love, my fair one," he said, taking her hand in his.

Leslie answered with a response from the Book of Ruth. "Entreat me not to leave thee, or to return from following after thee: for wither thou goest, I will go. And where thou lodgest, I will lodge. Thy people shall be my people, and thy God my God."

Reverend Martin began the vows. "Bradley, wilt

thou have this woman to be thy wife, and wilt thou
pledge thy troth to her, in all love and honor, in all duty
and service, in all faith and tenderness, to live with
her, and cherish her, according to the ordinance of
God, in the holy bond of marriage?"

Brad spoke very clearly. He had no doubts. "I
will."

"Leslie, wilt thou have this man to be thy husband, and wilt thou pledge thy troth to him, in all love
and honor, in all duty and service, in all faith and tenderness, to live with him, and cherish him, according to
the ordinance of God, in the holy bond of marriage?"

Leslie lifted her face to Brad's and replied in a
heartfelt whisper. "I will."

The pastor then turned to Jennifer and Stuart.
"Mr. and Mrs. Brooks, do you give your blessing to
this union for your daughter Leslie?"

How Brad wished his own parents, who had been
unable to leave Quincy at this time, could have been
there as Leslie's mother and father answered in unison,
"I do."

"Bradley and Leslie, your wedding vows?"

Brad began them. "I, Brad, take thee, Leslie, to
be my wedded wife. And I do promise and covenant,
before God and these witnesses, to be thy loving and
faithful husband, to have and to hold, from this day
forward, for better, for worse, for richer, for poorer, in
sickness and in health, to love and to cherish—till
death us do part."

And then Leslie. "I, Leslie, take thee, Brad, to be
my wedded husband. And I do promise and covenant,
before God and these witnesses, to be thy loving and
faithful wife, to have and to hold, from this day forward, for better, for worse, for richer, for poorer, in
sickness and in health, to love and to cherish—till
death us do part."

Brad turned to Greg for the ring. "As a symbol of
my vows," he said, slipping the shining gold band on the
third finger of her soft, left hand, "I give you this
ring."

Reverend Martin held up a heavy silver chalice.
"Wine," he said, addressing the wedding guests, "symbolizes the gift of life. It represents new life and the giving of life." He offered it first to Les, and then to Brad, and as they sipped in turn, he continued speaking. "As Brad and Leslie drink from their wedding cup, may they experience not only the presence of God, but also the spiritual union that will bind them one to the other as man and wife."

The next part of the ceremony contained two rituals Les had borrowed from her sister's wedding. Together, the wedding couple took up lighted tapers and turned to a candle standing at the side of the altar, lighting it simultaneously.

"As Leslie and Brad light the one candle with these two tapers," the pastor said, "may their lives also become one in the sharing of the love and trust they have promised to each other. And may the relighting of this candle on future anniversaries be a symbolic reminder of this vow—a vow which, with the grace of God, will remain strong until only death separates them."

Brad and Les each then took a rose from a crystal vase and offered them to Chris, who in turn presented them to Stuart and Jennifer.

"As God has nurtured these roses," Reverend Martin said to the Brookses, "so you as parents have nurtured these children. Take them as a symbol of the child you are today giving away in marriage."

And at last he spoke the words that truly joined them. "And now, forasmuch as Bradley and Leslie have consented together in holy wedlock, and have witnessed the same before God and this company, and thereto have pledged their troth each to the other, and have declared the same by joining hands, and by the giving and receiving of a ring, and further by dedicating themselves through the celebration of holy communion, I pronounce that they are husband and wife together. And what God hath joined together, let no man put asunder."

As Mrs. Bradley Eliot lifted her veil with trembling fingers, her husband smiled into her eyes and gave her a kiss straight from his bursting heart.

ABOUT THE AUTHOR

DEBORAH SHERWOOD was born in Tulsa, Oklahoma, but moved to Hollywood while still in her teens to pursue a career as an actress and model. A strong interest in writing led her to New York City some years later, where she wrote several nonfiction books, including *A Redhead in Red Square* and *The Story of a Happy Witch,* and penned some five hundred magazine articles. While interviewing actors for daytime fan magazines, she developed an interest in soap opera which eventually led to her going to work as a scriptwriter on some of the shows themselves. Currently a member of ABC's "General Hospital" writing team, she recently pulled up her New York roots and returned to California, to live and work amid the peace and tranquility of a remote beach community.

Barbara Cartland

The world's bestselling author of romantic fiction.
Her stories are always captivating tales of intrigue,
adventure and love.

☐	THE TEARS OF LOVE	2148	$1.25
☐	THE DEVIL IN LOVE	2149	$1.25
☐	THE ELUSIVE EARL	2436	$1.25
☐	THE BORED BRIDEGROOM	6381	$1.25
☐	JOURNEY TO PARADISE	6383	$1.25
☐	THE PENNILESS PEER	6387	$1.25
☐	NO DARKNESS FOR LOVE	6427	$1.25
☐	THE LITTLE ADVENTURE	6428	$1.25
☐	LESSONS IN LOVE	6431	$1.25
☐	THE DARING DECEPTION	6435	$1.25
☐	CASTLE OF FEAR	8103	$1.25
☐	THE GLITTERING LIGHTS	8104	$1.25
☐	A SWORD TO THE HEART	8105	$1.25
☐	THE MAGNIFICENT MARRIAGE	8166	$1.25
☐	THE RUTHLESS RAKE	8240	$1.25
☐	THE DANGEROUS DANDY	8280	$1.25
☐	THE WICKED MARQUIS	8467	$1.25
☐	LOVE IS INNOCENT	8505	$1.25
☐	THE FRIGHTENED BRIDE	8780	$1.25
☐	THE FLAME IS LOVE	8887	$1.25

Buy them at your local bookseller or use this handy coupon:

EMILIE LORING

Women of all ages are falling under the enchanting spell Emilie Loring weaves in her beautiful novels. Once you have finished one book by her, you will surely want to read them all.

☐	NO TIME FOR LOVE	2228	$1.25
☐	LOVE WITH HONOR	2237	$1.25
☐	BEYOND THE SOUND OF GUNS	2249	$1.25
☐	ACROSS THE YEARS	2278	$1.25
☐	FAIR TOMORROW	2287	$1.25
☐	WITH THIS RING	2294	$1.25
☐	WHAT THEN IS LOVE	2302	$1.25
☐	WE RIDE THE GALE	2320	$1.25
☐	UNCHARTED SEAS	2330	$1.25
☐	FORSAKING ALL OTHERS	2382	$1.25
☐	HOW CAN THE HEART FORGET	2390	$1.25
☐	TO LOVE AND TO HONOR	2391	$1.25
☐	TODAY IS YOURS	2394	$1.25
☐	THE SHINING YEARS	2410	$1.25
☐	HILLTOPS CLEAR	2496	$1.25
☐	STARS IN YOUR EYES	6618	$1.25

Buy them at your local bookstore or use this handy coupon for ordering: